The Jirí Chronicles & Other Fictions

by

Debra Di Blasi

The University of Alabama Press
Tuscaloosa, Alabama 35487-0380

First Edition

Published by FC2, an imprint of the University of Alabama Press, with support provided by Florida State University and the Publications Unit of the Department of English at Illinois State University

Address all editorial inquiries to: Fiction Collective Two, Florida State University, c/o English Department, Tallahassee, FL 32306-1580

∞
The paper on which this book is printed meets the minimum requirements of American National Standard for Information Sciences—Permanence of Paper for Printed Library Materials, ANSI Z39.48–1984

Library of Congress Cataloging-in-Publication Data
Di Blasi, Debra, 1957-
The Jiri chronicles & other fictions / by Debra Di Blasi. — 1st ed.
p. cm.
"Fiction Collective Two"
ISBN-13: 978-1-57366-136-2 (pbk. : alk. paper)
ISBN-10: 1-57366-136-8 (pbk. : alk. paper)
I. Title. II. Title: Jiri chronicles and other fictions.
PS3554.I1735J57 2007
813'.54—dc22
2006021471

Cover Design: Lou Robinson
Book Design: Debra Di Blasi
Typefaces: Cochin, Fritz Quadrata, Gill Sans
Produced and printed in the United States of America

Acknowledgements

Colossal thanks to FC2, especially R. M. Berry, Brenda Mills, Lance Olsen, and Doug Rice for their intelligence and support. Ditto to Dan Waterman and all at University of Alabama Press. Special gratitude to the Christopher Isherwood Foundation for awarding me the James C. McCormick Fellowship in Fiction.

And thanks to editors, curators, et al., who first published or exhibited these works, some in slightly different form:

The Iowa Review for publishing "Czechoslovakian Rhapsody Sung to the Accompaniment of Piano" and, later, "Glauke's Gown." Special warm thanks to editor David Hamilton for his early interest in *The Jirí Chronicles* that got the waxy ball rolling.

Notre Dame Review for "Oops. Sorry" and "Haunted," and their *NOW/THEN* anthology for republishing "Czechoslovakian Rhapsody Sung to the Accompaniment of Piano." Big thanks to editor/writer Steve Tomasula for aiding and abetting.

The Melic Review for "Ways a Father Dies" and "Fist," especially ghost-of-my-past poet/editor Jim Zola for inviting Jirí Cêch to guest edit the Spring 2004 poetry section.

First Intensity for "William Wesley Pickens, Jr., 1942," "Donald Eugene Pickens, 1943" and "Family Reunion, 1941."

Chelsea for "Sister Sister Sister Sister."

Poetry Midwest for "The Last Mare."

Rhapsoidia for "Sparrows" and for the Pushcart Prize nomination.

&NOW Festival of Innovative Writing and Art and, later, Riverfront Readings and The Writers Place (gratitude to poet Phyllis Becker) for supporting the presentation of "In Case You Haven't Noticed I'm Not Wearing Any Clothes."

The Prague Review for "Exiles" and "Blue."

Big Ugly Review for "Seed" – plus thanks for selecting it as a first-place winner of *And So It Begins...* flash fiction competition.

Show+Tell anthology, published by Potpourri Publications, for "Mrs. Conner and Her Six Children, 1883," "William Wesley Pickens Sr., 1910," "Charles Elliot Pickens, 1940," and "Devon D. Pickens, 1957."

Clay Palm Review for "Blue."

Poet and critic H.L. Hix for writing a witty essay introducing Jirí Cêch in the 24: 2 issue of *Pleiades*.

David Hughes of Urban Culture Project and Davin Watne of The Dirt Gallery for exhibiting The Jirí Chronicles multimedia installation.

The late, lovely artist Lester Goldman and HammerPress for publishing "Mannequins: Sketches of Marriage" in Lester's fine art book, *Welcome to the Ragball*.

H&R Block ArtSpace for first exhibiting the ad fictions "Face It," "Life Is Scary," and "Think Again," and for exhibiting the samizdat, *Who The Hell Is The Real Jirí Cêch?* in *Making Meaning: The Artist Book*.

For their role in helping to legitimize the bastard Jirí Cêch, thanks to Wayne Miller, Kevin Prufer, Eric Williamson (all of *Pleiades*), and Jeanne Ouellette.

Also by Debra Di Blasi

Ugly Town

Drought & Say What You Like

Prayers of an Accidental Nature

for Mark
bulwark against madness

Contents

Snapshots:
A Genealogy In Flight

Mrs. Conner and Her Six Children
1883

I love sepia photographs, warm brown like clayey earth, earth better for bare feet in summer than crops or pastures. And it was like that for them: some things better for this than that, and their near poverty baked into the lines of their brows—even the youngest scowling at memories of a hard winter or too-long summer where nothing they tried worked all the way. Corn puny, calves stillborn, broken plow, and rat dead in the well.

Still, she gathered them all together, made them spit-shine their shoes and slick back their hair, iron the lace and ribbon the curls, hold their heads high like the royals they'd never be.

She spent a season's wages on that photograph: warm, warm brown to soften the hardness of their lives, so that when he—*coward husband, bastard father*—opened up the envelope and pulled out the photograph and held it in his hands gone white-soft from the ease of his new life, he'd think them somehow prosperous and proud, the lines in their brows not the deep-plowed furrows of failure but an indictment of him—*coward bastard, father husband*—who had stood at the door and waved, and lied, saying he'd send for them soon, soon they'd all be rich and happy.

William Wesley Pickens, Sr.
1910

A new century was coming on, already arrived in the shape of tractors plowing the rolling fields that would be his—the tractors, the fields—and every horse would be bred for looks from now on, and speed. That's right! Who needed strong backs when there was iron and steel and engines like unbreakable hearts.

Unlike his: *Chelsea* broken here and there across the county where he rode from house to house, courting the daughters of men who coveted his black soils, but the daughters running off with older boys—soldiers and sailors and thieves—who'd take them far from the heat and sweat of Missouri farms. Except one daughter whose name was Grace and who was grace and so he married her.

Oh, yes!

A new century coming, and somewhere in his affable intelligence he could smell its promise: pungent and sweet as the sweat of flanks slick with summer. And the long ride through fecund pastures where grasshoppers whirred and rose like airplanes—what a swell invention!

In his eager fallible optimism he believed even war would mean progress: killing machines killing with swift efficiency, cleaner than before: men dying in a flash of white light, screamless—no clatter of hooves, no sneer or cry. And all this in the name of peace that would be irrevocable, he thought, as the wind is irrevocable in its flight across fields where he flew on his plain strong-back horse at the end of each lonely day, sun beckoning from the horizon of his future perfect. And his unborn sons who would be pilots, who would kill swiftly, efficiently, cleanly from the white light of skies. And a world he thought he knew without end.

Charles Elliot Pickens
1940

He had not yet gone to war, though as youngest and wildest he already felt the itch of it. It wasn't that he wanted to kill. Hell, killing was nothing and not so hard—he'd done it plenty: chickens, goats, sheep, cattle, deer. But never a man. No, not a man. It wasn't something he looked forward to when he looked forward to war. But he could do it, he was pretty damn sure. Could kill a man if necessary, if a bayonet pointed in his direction, if his own rifle pointed in theirs. If someone hollered, "Shoot!"

Damn Japs, he'd spit later, on Guadalcanal, where he finally landed in the infantry. And, yes, war was all he'd imagined and more: the stink of fear so thick it fell on the tongue. More incriminating than the stink of his own shit in his pants when the shelling came. Or his breath of stomach rotted on lousy food and too many smokes and unending dread that spoiled and soiled the pristine island air. Or the nightmares of his best buddy who spoke them aloud in his sleep, low-moaning litany for a Methodist God too distant now to forgive anyone: God, too, like a dream gone awry.

But, going back before he was changed into the living guilty, the guilty lucky, unharmed and safely home while half the others died or came home in half...back when he stood young and wild on the lawn in his linen trousers and white tee-shirt, so white the sun hid inside it the way it hid inside the Guadalcanal sky, glowing white with its terrible secret: *War or not, God will take you young, Charlie, just for the sake of irony.*

And so it was: car crash on a back road, and he the driver who raced stock cars after the war just to taunt death whose hands, he thought, were visible but were not.

Family Reunion
1941

These are the ones I don't know. Faces I don't see when I look in the mirror. The way I see the wide pupils of my father's eyes, my mother's quick grin, and lashes thick and black spilled down even to a nephew newborn who'll learn to flutter them or fold them or hold them still to get what he wants, and he'll get it one way or another. So much weight in lashes weightless as they fall onto a cheek or pillow or page or photograph. Threads of a flag unfurled over the rampart of the eyes.

Most of these eyes are dead by now. Time-sucked dry of their ocular fluids. But see how they shine here: these with arrogance, these with joy, these with smarts, these with shyness so deep it draws the arms across the belly and crosses them there taut and fearful in their worry of the world's dangers. And there will be plenty of dangers, and most of them in the heart, and none of them fatal except one.

This distant dead cousin, nameless, she cocks her head as if listening to a voice off to the left, just out of the camera's range, whispering, *Look hard, look harder. See there in the future without you eyes that will not know your name, your story, your dreams like the ash of sleep and so many fancies that proved barren as the stunted tree behind you, uprooted and burned long before she will be born. Tell her who does not know what it means to live your one modest life, to work so hard to forget the forgettable things, bleach the stains of love that bled from your fingertips, watch your hair stop curling and go gray.*

Listen, listen. You've just this moment. Quick! Tell me your name, your story, your place in my history already resembling your own. Tell me now. Before all the silver of your slanting glance is burned away by the light.

William Wesley Pickens, Jr.
1942

I wish this to be my last image of you, Uncle: the eponymous son on leave from the war. Uniform clean and crisp and too short in the arms for you'd grown since leaving the father frowning proud beside you, grown taller in ways he would never comprehend. Never your brother (my father) too, standing opposite you as in life—on leave but dressed civilian as if he couldn't wait for the nightmare to end, and he couldn't but would. And you couldn't wait to return.

I wish.

And your Air Force cap cocked upon the cocky head of a pilot who knew things already, already knew you couldn't be grounded by women or jobs or life. Would keep moving, your own wind and weather, flying everlasting until the pretty word rose up before you—*everlasting!*—like the Giza pyramids you saw once, from above, and said *My God,* not as a curse but a sudden confession of belief that you hid like a wicked secret for fifty years while uncountable miles slipped under you: abalone rivers and patchwork fields and cities spreading from sea to shining sea.

Ah, you flying everlasting beyond the voices of angels in the sky—what other voices could they have been? Heaven, you said, not the hell of farm dirt with its own tongue, devil tongue calling you down and home. Gravity, you knew too, was real.

I wish but cannot. Rather, I see now that death was always there, in your lips parted not in a smile but a complaint yet unspoken, your eyes hidden in shadow while gazing past it at African skies free of flak like generous lovers who appeared at your wake, all mascara and ruby lips and eyes shadowed in sky-blue and bosoms lavish of light and endless, and a pilot's freefall into them the ultimate consummation: marriage of dream and dream.

All in one piece, I wish. No holes to be patched up at day's end, life's end, the way the mortician patched your forehead where you aimed the gun and the bullet flew into a mind so angry with cancer and age and bitterness and gravity's last laugh that there was nothing to do really, really nothing else but to make it empty: eyes gazing everlasting inward at the beauty of sky blown clean.

Donald Eugene Pickens
1943

No wonder I love handsome men. My father resembled Tyrone Power. That's what my mother told me and I see now that it's true. Why she married him, she said. Why she dreamed fever dreams of him when he was absent, and how the dreams were never as fine as the real thing.

My father was the real thing. The way he wore his Air Force uniform, seams pressed to knife blades. The way he posed for the camera, careful how he draped his arms, crossed his legs, laid his cap at his feet on the lawn that stretched backward into infinity, past the Welshmen and the Scotsmen who caught their women in nets of black-eyed glances. Back, back, beyond the Devonshire hills that would soon catch my father in their wet green gaze, ease his fears, solace him before those last terrible flights into Germany, and the screaming white flak, and the cell-sickness of terror.

The day after his best friend was shot down over a black land speckled in flame, he returned old to the English hills, though he was only 23, and vowed to a God he never trusted that he would forfeit the metal glint of flight and money for a parcel of his own green land if God would just—*Please, God, in your limitless heaven!*—see him through the next mission and so through the war and bring him home again across the water to suckle at America's breast.

Amen.

Not a limb lost, not a bullet taken, not even a scratch or blemish to his movie star face. Instead: a soul pierced and scarred by what he concluded in hindsight was the cowardice of prayer. And in summer, every summer, the rolling hills of his Missouri land green and wet, it seems, now and forever, with mourning.

Devon D. Pickens
1957

It's quite obvious: You were happy before I came along and spoiled it all. That's what I'm told. That's what I see in photos of a child whose countenance shifts so radically from delight to dour I think I must have been born without a soul and survived only by stealing yours.

Soulless child, angry child. Named after the English town whence our father took off in a Flying Fortress to drop bombs over Dresden and kill children like you who must have thought the flak and whistle were stars inventing new constellations to forever mark the pain of this bloody century.

Your pain, this century, what a legacy! Fisted and gritting against life. A hundred schoolyard battles, a hundred barroom brawls, and all the doves and coons and deer you fell to prove no one's cut you down. Not yet. Though I know you sense the end—animal smell heavy—when you're flying your own fortress at night, high above a landscape of timber and pastures that give you nothing if not a placid marker of where you'll one day land.

Dear brother, I give you back your soul this night when stars are fixed and silent. When death is someone else's luck. When catfish are indeed jumping, and coyotes are yapping, and your family is a comfort and close. I give you a new millennium, new world to come—hope for all our angry souls. Let's you and I absolve the world its pain, and honor the dust and ash that brought us safely home, here along these warm lake shores, night into dawn.

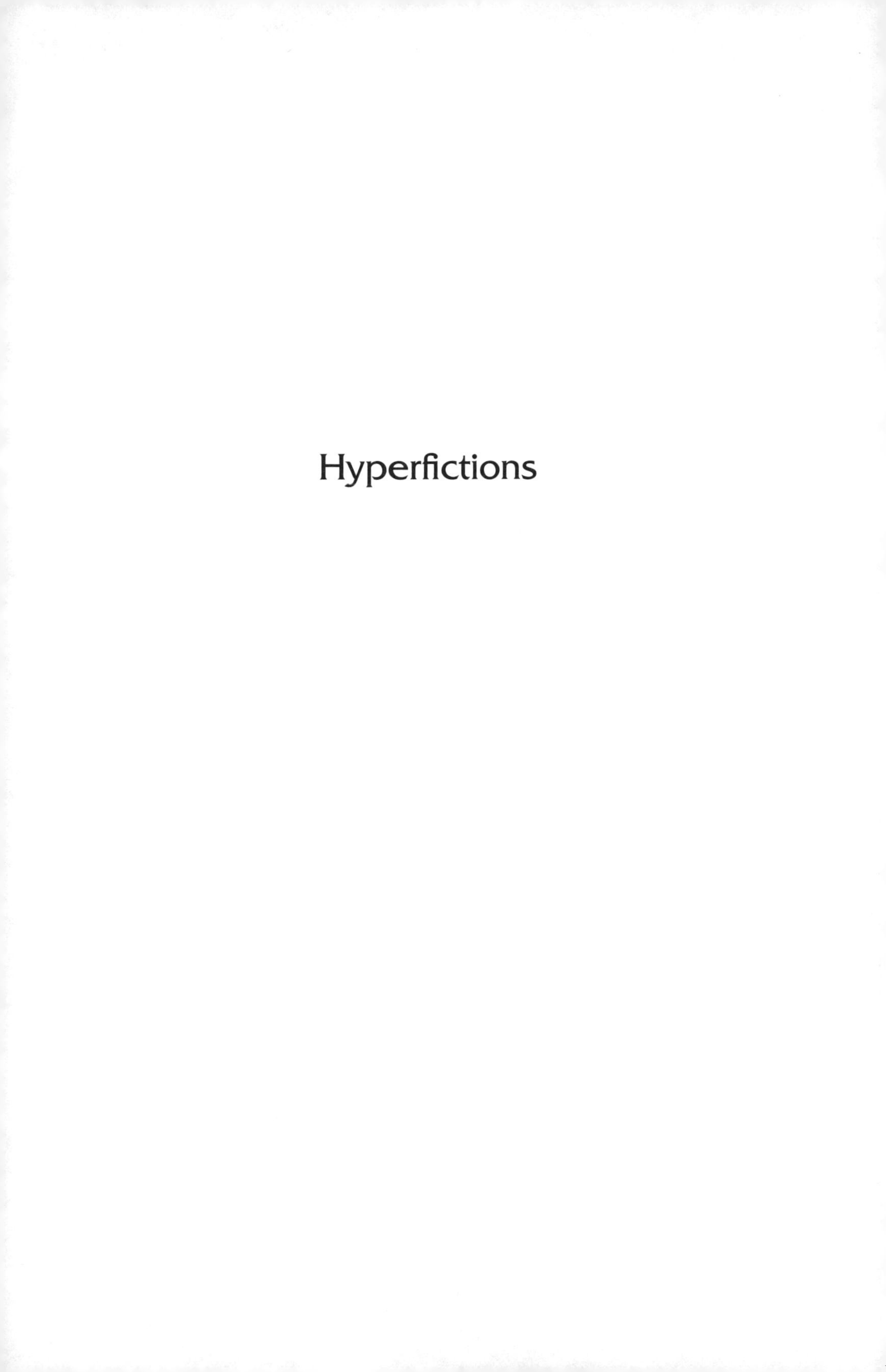

Hyperfictions

Ways a Father Dies

one

In this case, it does not happen quickly. He only complains the air is thin, tinged maybe with pollen or smoke or lead. Indeed, a leaden weight on his chest wakes him every damn night. Like a big cat crouched, he says, and wet. Like the cougar he once saw bowed in a creek bed, coughing up bone and fur. Bad meat, poison meat, meat of the future where all cougars moved away north or were shot by land developers. Those pretty hills, he says, someday they'll just be houses full of misery, of not quite content, never heart-fed. And you, old man, staring at a century's bloodshot eyes? You? *I've lived my time,* he says, *I've worked my gullet raw spitting up bone.* He coughs blood into his hand to prove it.

two

Winter, there's no heat in his feet. Beneath thick yellow toenails: a shade of blue like crushed lilacs and bug chitin mixed. He killed bugs when he was young and kept killing for decades: pigs, calves, mice, squirrels, rabbits, muskrats. Even a lame horse. Even an old dog. Then one day he watched a half-eaten frog crawl toward a pond, no hind legs, a clouded eye. The hawk that'd chewed and dropped it stood perched in the nearby elm, furious hungry. *Well go on,* the father shouted, *get 'em before he reaches water!* But the hawk only unsettled its feathers. When the frog finally reached the muddy bank, the fetid pond, a patch of algae teeming with worms, the father was emancipated from his past grown hard and foreign in every shining surface. He felt, intensely, each creature's obliging life. This winter his legs too will disappear. Hawks will watch him crawling across snow. Not toward home, no, just crawling.

three

The children rarely visit. All right, they're not children now, but he can't think of them as adults, either—their voices still whine with need. No one cares that he keenly hears the silence squealing through the house. And him a heel-step behind, stalking the empty rooms, sniffing for anything that might accompany him into his lonely death. That scent of newborn, of smoke or chocolate. *If there's time,* he says aloud, to nobody, *I'll die here on this wooden chair so there's less stink when they find me.* He considers the offer, then replies, *No, you'll die on the unplowed land. Let the coyotes and maggots clean their plate of you. Let the children think you fled to some park in the desert where all the old forgotten die in concert, holding hands.*

four

Death is not the end of his body. A body that means nothing to everyone now. Including, especially, his doctor who sees only money in the slow flesh-rot. Nope. Death is the end of five children's voices playing on a hot summer night upon a rural lawn mown tidy. It exists only in memory, forever, as long as he is. Memory saturated with humidity and the unstinking sweat of a five-year-old's twig-twining arm around his sun-scalded neck, and a moon wholly tender in expression like his brother dead two lifetimes now but blessed risen that August night fifty goddamn years ago. Risen and shining down on this sealed moment, benevolent as dreams ascended from the breathlessness of fading. Every one so Jesus-real he reaches down and yanks a fistful of grass already starting to dew. Smells it, sweet and pliable as love. His hands bent now always with this gesture of age and grace.

Sister Sister Sister Sister

Begin. I begin. This. I begin this st

st

st
st

st st st

ssssssssssssssssssssss

sssstory about

mmmmmmmmmmmm

mmmmmmmmmmmmmmmy my my sister.

WHY IS THAT SO HARD TO SAY?

I haven't seen her for oh I don't know maybe thirty years. She must be old by now. Older, at least. I must be older too, though when I remember my sister I am fourteen. But of course I am not. I am fifty. My hair is gray under the red dye. My sister is fifty-two. Unless she is dead. I've heard she is alive. Rumors.

BECAUSE I STUTTER. RATHER, I USED TO. BACK WHEN I KNEW MY SISTER. I QUIT STUTTERING WHEN SHE RAN AWAY FROM HOME. IT WAS LIKE SHE TOOK THE GAPS WITH HER. TUCKED THEM IN THE DIRT-BLUE BACKPACK ALONG WITH THE OTHER STUFF SHE STOLE: DAD'S POCKET KNIFE, MOM'S PERFUME AND LIPSTICK, THE DOG'S VACCINATION TAGS, MONEY. AND MY STUTTER.

THE SPEECH PATHOLOGIST SAID IT WAS BECAUSE I FELT INFERIOR TO MY SISTER. "SHADED," HE SAID. AS IF SHE WAS AN OAK AND I WAS GRASS.

Oh, and she took the neighbor boy's marijuana.

I DIDN'T FEEL INFERIOR TO MY SISTER. JUST UNRELATED. LIKE SHE WAS ADOPTED. LIKE HER REAL PARENTS WERE ECCENTRIC INTELLECTUALS LIVING IN PARIS OR SOMETHING. ME, I WAS BORN OF DAD AND MOM. THEY'RE FROM KANSAS.

Stoner.
Whore.
Thief.
Pretty.
Smart.
Long blonde hair.
Straight hair.
Perfect hippie chick.
My sister.

Haight-Asbury. 1972. Where she ran to. *Lookin' for life, baby sis!*— what she wrote in fat hollow letters on the back of a postcard of the Golden Gate Bridge. Peace sign drawn in lipstick. My mother's probably. And the words, *Keep On Truckin Man,* in somebody else's handwriting. Some guy's, I'm sure.

Derinda says, "I hear your sister gave Robert Martin a blow job."

I ask, "What's a blow job?"

Derinda says, "God you're so stupid!"

I ask, "But what is it?"

Derinda rolls her eyes and says, "It's when a girl puts her mouth over a guy's wiener and licks it and sucks on it like a Tootsie Pop until all of his stuff comes gushing out."

I ask, "What stuff?"

Derinda rolls her eyes and says, "His wad, you know, his cum his gism his juice his—"

"Semen?" I ask.

Derinda looks at me suspiciously. "How'd you know that word if you don't know what a blow job is?"

"Biology class," I say.

"Oh," says Derinda. "I got a D in biology."

Derinda had an older sister, Debbie, who knew my sister. They were in the same class together. But they were not friends. Debbie was wild and mean. She hit people. Once she hit my sister because my sister was pretty. That was the only reason. Debbie liked Joe Borden but Joe Borden liked my sister and said so to Debbie. When Debbie asked him why, he told her, "Cuz she's pretty." So next time Debbie saw my sister, she punched her in the mouth. Fortunately my sister had good strong teeth and none of them broke. But she had a scar on the inside of her lower lip for a year. Maybe always.

I DON'T KNOW.

She stopped talking about it. And then she was gone.

I DON'T KNOW WHERE MY SISTER IS. NO ONE KNOWS.

NO. NO. SOMEONE KNOWS. UNLESS SHE'S DEAD. I DON'T THINK SHE'S DEAD.

THERE ARE RUMORS.

In 1996 Troy Johnson said he saw her maybe at a burger joint just outside L.A. three years earlier. He was on his way back from somewhere he wouldn't say and stopped in for a bite to eat. He said there was this woman sitting in a booth with some fat fuck Harley sort. Said he never would've noticed them except he heard a yelp and looked back over his shoulder and saw the fat fuck with his fat hand around the woman's wrist turning her arm sideways and backwards like the winner in an arm wrestling match. Said the woman looked exactly like my sister, only older. Said he kept staring at her until the fat fuck got up and came over to his table and said, "You gotta problem?" Troy left. Without asking her name. But he swears, he swears it was her.

Troy is addicted to gambling.

TROY WAS A YEAR OLDER THAN MY SISTER AND SMART ENOUGH TO GO AWAY TO A GOOD SCHOOL IN THE EAST. HE STUDIED HISTORY THERE FOR YEARS THEN ENDED UP IN L.A. TEACHING AT SOME COLLEGE, NOT A BIG ONE. USED TO FLY INTO LAS VEGAS EVERY WEEKEND TO GAMBLE. UNTIL HE LOST SO MUCH MONEY HE HAD TO DRIVE. THEN HE LOST HIS CAR. LOST HIS JOB.

But Troy swears it was her. Still pretty, he said, but weathered. Desert suck, that's what he called it. Desert sucks all the wetness from you same way poverty does. Poverty, desert, they make you old.

So does gambling, by the look of Troy.

The only boy I ever slept with. Who said, afterward, "You're not your sister."

SHE'D BE OLD BY NOW—2002—LIKE ME.

When I dream about her she's no age at all. Or maybe all ages. Like how I remember her the day she was leaving: tossing her hair, waving, laughing, *Break on through to the other side, baby sis,* and then gone. Like how I remember her in Troy's story: sucked dry. And in the dreams she's always doing something ordinary, like washing dishes or brushing her hair or shaving her legs, except there's grace in each act, remarkable grace, as if everything she did was impeccable, choreographed and rehearsed.

But that wasn't how she was.

She was she was

my sister shhhhhh shhhhhhhhhh

shhhh she

was.

My parents never mention her name. But they think of her: Mom's pinched lips when she's wiping down the kitchen counter. Dad's faraway stare when he's standing on the porch drinking a beer. She was his favorite. Mom's favorite too.

NOW THEY'RE LEFT WITH ME.

I'M LEFT WITH THEM.

Sometimes at night I go to her room and lie down on her bed and pretend I'm her at fourteen, making up my mind to leave. When I open my mouth to speak only singing escapes.

Seed

I'd never seen a tree on fire before. Yet now, at the bottom of the old man's pond, I imagined pine trees burning. Smell of bitter sap and flame. Nesting crows flying into the wind. Smoke roiling. He'd tied my wrists and ankles with baling twine, put a burlap sack over my head and tossed me from the back of his pickup into the fetid water. I suspect he drove away then, not even a backward glance over his bony shoulder. He'd always said, *What's past is past. Pain your neck twistin back-eyed at it.* And then he'd spit, as if defiling history. His. Mine. Everyone's. Eventually the spit dried to nothing, proving him right. I never doubted him. Never questioned him but once. It was wrong, I said, to kill a worker for stealing, even if he was a vagrant. *Ain't,* said the old man. And he looked at me like I was a tick he'd just picked from his scalp, filled fat with his blood. Half was true: his blood in my veins, mixed with blood of a mother I couldn't remember. After she died he burned the only photos of her. Not to forget, but to appease his rage. *Damn her to hell for dying on me,* he said when things went from bad to worse. As if she could have saved him. Saved me. No. We were damned from the seed root, all of us. Eyes too close together and brows low and teeth twisted in our mouths. Nothing but pine trees on a mountainside waiting for the lightning bolt that would set us all ablaze. Let me burn, I thought, here in the bottom of his muddy pond. Let my smoke rise out of water and follow these blessed winds. I'll rain down somewhere far and pretty. Take root. Remember nothing but the sound of crows in fiery treetops.

Long After Winter:
Galesburg, Illinois

This canceled day with tight wind reminds her she was such a pretty angry girl red temper flaming like her hair her lips the boys loved songs passing through that fleshy heartshape love songs though she did not want them those punching bragging boys she loved only the pale young man with one leg shorter and a dent in his brow where shrapnel slapped flat his skull made him stupid some said they laughed but she knew his gangly gift clemency for all things beautiful he sang weeping on stage alongside her pretty wild those days when theatre troupes came to town with lights shining like a come-hither fingernail she curled around into his nape sweat they kissed good-bye he said if you can't run away so now angry this blank wind sixty years blown by wait she dreams twitching wait for me.

Sparrows

Poetry ought to have a mother as well as a father.
—Virginia Woolf

THE LAND KNEW AND THE AIR KNEW:

Be still before the storm, still before the quake. And the creatures knew, too: A sparrow sped low across the field and lit on a slender branch, knotting herself in a tight ball like a fist against water, the way water becomes hard as flesh on bone when you strike it. The way she—the sparrow, my mother—was struck by life.

I USED TO LIE IN BED WITH MY HAND OVER MY HEART waiting for it to stop beating. There were so many ways to die, I already knew.

Farm girl, tomboy, broomstick legs and goose neck craned toward the widening world, curiosity glinting in my frog eyes, I'd seen death a hundred times already: pig death, calf death, dog death, spider death, possum, coon, carp, flea...

But no death worse than a woman's living death.

I USED TO LIE IN BED WITH MY HAND OVER MY HEART thinking of my mother's life. She had been beautiful. Five children and a home without plumbing and a husband angry had made her tired. When she sat in a room alone, knees tucked under her bottom, eyes gazing out the window past the fields of fescue and corn, past the present into the past, her voice hummed like a ghost's sorrowful lament. She'd had dreams. Folks told her they were impossible. She believed folks.

I DID NOT WANT TO DIE IN LIFE.

My broken heart broken for my mother. She swept the floor and told me, "Don't do what I've done," then swept her hand across the landscape of cattle and crops and told me, "There's more, so much more." And in her hand one day a pile of white pills and in her heart a yearning only for the end of things.

THE LAND KNEW AND THE AIR KNEW

and so there was such a yawning stillness in that moment gazing at pills like white confetti, bits of yearning bleached clean of color. And her other hand smelling of bleach as she held it to her nose and looked at the floor, at the cracked linoleum bleached as clean as she could get it. Spotless, sure. Until. Until, she imagined, the first footfall of the youngest child tottering across it, softly crying, "Mommy?"

Dear Kids, There is nothing I can say to make this what I am doing okay for you. I am just

— Did I ever tell you about my friend Sue?
— Yes.
— She killed herself when she was just 26.
— Why?
— Because she had no voice.
— What does that mean?
— She lost her voice!
— Literally?
— Yes. She had dreams. Her dreams got smaller as she got older. She wanted so much more, you know. To sing. So much more.
— You've said.
— Her voice got smaller with her dreams. Like a whisper. Like a child's whisper. Until it went out.
— No voice.
— None. Then she died.

THE AIR KNEW, TOO
and she thought perhaps her pain had made her deaf. Such silence! She turned her head just as the earth began to tremble. The walls trembling, too, as if the house, her life were tumbling down around her—dishes crashing to the floor, chairs scraping, pots and pans and cans the percussion behind the odd squeal of wood, crunch of stucco. Earth. Quake.

When your heart pounds at night in bed it's as if the earth's convulsing under your spine.

SHE DROPPED THE PILLS AND RAN.

She said: "Find your voice."
She said: "Live."

The children—we—were standing in the near pasture staring up at elms swaying in the windless air. Mouths agape like baby birds waiting for the mother sparrow to come back to the nest. So to speak. She came back, running. Gathered us under her wings and repeated over and over, "You will not, at least. You, at least, will not." Until the quake subsided, shuddering once and hard again, then never. And the trees grew still. The sparrows sang. Flew.

SOON
she'd start talking to me about Paris. Sing French songs.
As if she'd ever been. As if she'd ever.

earth
quake

The Last Mare

The day after my mother died—heart still as winter—my father gathered the mares from the west paddock and one by one shot them with his .38. Once behind the left ear. Twice if their twitching persisted.

It was not the sun I saw glinting in the last mare's eye but fear. The stench of death's sweat filled her nostrils and there was no escape, though she bucked and kicked at the wooden chute until it splintered. Splintered but held.

And I hoped after the last mare dropped and bled onto the mud black with bleeding—my eyes closed tight against the terrible light of death's glance—hoped that my father would turn the trigger on himself and put him out of my misery.

He did not.

It is eighty-one years past and my father is long dead and I am old and tired, tired of it all. Yet look at me here: See how I still buck in my sleep, buck and kick, kicking fiercely now against the fierce approaching light.

Mannequins: Sketches of Marriage

ear

I wake each morning to your left ear. Think of the sea. Glint of silver. Abalone washed onto a warm bed of sand. I dream beaches, kelp, waves cresting and collapsing into a flood-whisper of pulse. My blood or yours, I can't say; we sleep so close in this cold. I hear the tide rise in your breath in my ear in a still winter room while you drift on the pearly current of daybreak, grateful but not surprised to be yet in love.

hand

When you drink wine from a stemmed glass you cradle the pellucid body as if it were an orchid damaged by touch. Every movement considered, displayed. I told you your hands were beautiful. You didn't believe me until another woman (old, sincere, nothing to prove but veracity) said the same. Now your hands are transformed: grace sprouting from wrists. Your eyes transformed too, watching a hand reach for a glass of wine like Adam reaching toward God and sentience, seeing neither God nor God's hand. Rather, your own flesh made holy reaching back in beauty.

body

You and I, our waters are not the same. What you know is surf and pull, great tides swinging on the moon's rope of light. I know ponds still as wet loam and just as black. Depths thick with moss and fleas, silt and roe. Miniature cosmos teeming. Ocean : Pond. When our bodies join, flesh to flesh, there's a churning like waters colliding. Roiling wet. Red Sea parting. Straight path to redemption, or at the very least bliss.

gristle

Already everything aches. Your knees, my back. Stiffness tames us to mannequins dressed and awkward in the world's window. It's the burden of height: *The bigger they are, the harder they fall.* Have we outgrown *Homo sapiens* optimal specifications? Should we have lumbered through our lives, not sped? Making love, shall we slide yet another pillow under my hips? Well. Entropy prevails. Gristle corrects the cadence. If we live forty more years we'll be as fixed as the horizon and just as flat.

foot

Your feet retain the tragedies they've walked through. Or kicked at. Or refused to bear. I run a fingernail over your sole and imagine misfortune's whorls cut a little deeper, twisted a little tighter than luck's. Luck, after all, is a kiss. It's night. I kiss your foot and fool myself into believing I know you better than I do, pressing on a callus, trying to make it yield. It holds.

Exiles

All I have now is your voice across a gulf of water. Beautiful voice, like water, but I've already used that analogy. Years ago. When your voice was younger and thus more like water, or less. Who can remember after all these years? And what point is there in remembering, anyway? Sword of pain. Pain in my heart. Pain in my ass, that is remembering. Therefore: *Voice like... Voice like... Voice like...*

But to hell with analogies.

It is your voice like your voice coming to me across a gulf of water and years and so many mistakes for both of us—more, I think, for you, but who's counting?

We are exiles. Though we have no grand excuse—Ovid with his Caesar Augustus. No, we are merely exiled, you and I, from each other. None to blame but ourselves. No, no, we cannot even blame ourselves for we were young then, susceptible to whim and fate. You more susceptible to whim, I more susceptible to fate.

"As if we're not susceptible now?" you say, grinning I am sure, your voice now a pool of water. Pool of light. Light of my life, gone all these years.

"Yes," I say, "but now we are wiser and we can brace ourselves against fate."

"Like against an oncoming car?" you ask, grinning again.

"No," I say, "an oncoming train."

"Moving very fast," you say.

"Very, very fast," I say.

And repeat: All I have now is your voice across a gulf across which rumors fly to me like winter geese: They say you are nearly civilized, that you eat mangoes every day, that you are more beautiful now than ever. I cannot imagine it. Yet I try: *Women collapsing at your feet.* But wait. That is memory.

"Women collapsed at your feet," I say.

"You're lonely," you say.

"And?" I say. "So?"

"Are you happy?" you ask.

"Yes," I reply. "It's just that sometimes I am not happy."

"Oh," you say.

Each time the phone rings I hope it is you twenty years ago saying, "Sorry I'm late. I'll be home soon."

It is late. Soon my home will fill up with night too thick for me to separate ink from page. And it will be late for you too—late and later, the sun rising first on your little island of exile: You will always know before I that tomorrow is indeed another day.

"Tomorrow is another day," you say.

"Indeed," I say.

Your voice like a mirror laid on ordinary dust. Dust of years. Years of exile. Unsweepable dust of years of exile from a man no longer but forever my husband. I am no longer allowed to say I love you. But I do, of course. Love you. Say it. Though you can't hear me across the indisputable gulf of water and years and errors between us.

Husband, here is my secret: You were the best year of my life.

Gulf of water. Water of words. Words like a gulf pretending to be a bridge into the past. The past is only memory cleared of debris. And these words—debris of the present—are going nowhere. Like me, like you. You'll stay on your island, I'll stay on my continent. Die here—again—these words on my lips:

You were the best year of my life.
You were the best year of my life.
You were the best year of my life…

Teeth heavy in my mouth.

Blue

Here in the cafe—near the music shop where he met the girl whom he loved first and well and who moved away soon after and became, after countable years and without much effort, a girl not often remembered—here he chooses the white table near the window opposite the blue table near the door. Each table in the cafe is painted a different color, a fact irritating in its predictability, as his life is predictable and thus irritating.

He sits at the white table and smokes cigarettes one after another as if breathing were a curse. And perhaps it is: breathing implying life or rather mere living. Mere. Much in the way a plant lives never having moved from its rooted spot or even swayed much without the assistance of wind or rain or passing animals. In other words: being alive without living, rooted to the spot, a spot not the best one, the one over there or over here, for example, where dreams manifest into reality. Rooted to a lesser spot, inferior, wretched.

What could be worse?

Well, today, coffee.

He drinks without tasting—the coffee's flavor overwhelmed by the dullness of his tongue, his tongue slightly swollen. *And for no good reason*, he thinks. A good reason such as a woman's sex: pink and moist, pulled wide by the hairs pulled back with thumbs and the tongue diving and licking, swelling over the course of her swelling, and who cares how long it takes her to come, or how much swelling?

His tongue swollen now for no good reason but the swelling of years and ennui with its settled posture of permanence: its sneer.

Assuming ennui causes lethargy, a dullness of the senses, a slow perpetual sinking heaviness of the body weighted by the death of the soul: corpse of light, heavy lit corpse. But no, not entirely lethargic. He shakes. His fingers, for example: involuntarily animated, shaking as they place a cigarette between his lips and his lips suck in slowly the smoke, smoking and smoking a cigarette held only inches from his lips so that the smallest effort is expended inhaling, therein the lethargy. Even the exhalations are careless, the smoke languidly curling out his mouth and nose over his fingers stained yellow by the curling smoke, the cigarette tip flaring slightly with each slight smoky exhalation.

Fuck me, he thinks. Not a shout but a sigh. A slow pulse: *fuck me, fuck me, fuck me...*

A speck of dried food, dark and greasy, on the edge of the blue table at which he stares remains what it is: a speck of dried food, static, though he wills it to move, fall off, be swept away, leaving an otherwise clean blue table perfectly clean.

Fuck me.

The speck remains.

The coffee, the cigarettes, the colored tables—all tasteless. Why choose the white table and not the blue? White: the equivalence of lacking, and he lacks. More than anything else, lacks is what he does best. Lacks: joy, hope, love, the cool of the blue table beneath his elbows, or his cheek should he wish to rest his head. Yet he chose the white. Why?

Why: Because, were he to sit at the blue table he would not be able to discern with such exactitude what it is he lacks. Even flying through a blue sky one cannot experience the sky's blueness. It remains a distant thing, unreachable, thus a greater tragedy than when viewed from the ground—a probable distance where there are no illusions, no delusions about touching the sky with one's fingers, curling around, latching hold of the sky's blueness with one's fingers. Fingers kept close now to the lips in order to smoke without ceasing like a fireman caught in a burning building full of smoke. (His father was a fireman. No, that is a lie. His father was a vagrant passing through his mother's life. No, that too is a lie. His father was, is—his father is not dead—vice president of a chemical company, a man who would sit at the blue table not because it is blue but because it is a table. *Well, fuck him.*)

And fuck me, too.

Choose the white table in order to better examine the blue. Command the speck of food to drop. Smoke the cigarette. Drink the coffee. Ignore the shaking fingers—though intentional ignorance highlights the thing to be ignored, doesn't it? *Doesn't it?*

Fuck me.

Fuck me. Please.

The girl at the music store, her hair a shimmering red-gold. What did she taste like? This: the blue table without the speck of dried food. Perfection, as only memory can invent with impeccable falseness. Perfection: a thing of the past. The past: ice breaking apart and flowing away from the shore. The girl looks up from the record rack and blushes, startled, and smiles. The feel of her red-gold hair between his fingers, the taste of her damp pink flesh on his swelling tongue breaks apart and slides away from the shore.

And so.

His cigarette smoked to the butt goes out on its own. He slackens his jaw to make room for his swollen tongue still swelling with dull time. Takes a last drink of coffee. Holds it in his mouth until it cools to his tongue's temperature. Spits the coffee back into the cup.

As he passes by the blue table on his way out the door he scrapes off the speck of dried food with his thumbnail. He leaves it there, under his thumbnail, and steps outside where the blue sky aches in the distance, comprehensible and intemporal—neither joy nor grief. He lights another cigarette, inhales, exhales the smoke nearly invisible in the brightness of the day...

And the sky absorbs everything unrooted.

He studies the speck of food beneath his nail, scrapes it out, flicks it at the sky—the blue distant sky like the past or an intolerably redundant future. He laughs, not audibly. And he is careful, in fact meticulous about which automobile he chooses to step in front of before crossing, but of course never crossing, the street.

Anonymous Children of Martin Luther...

1. (...who was anti-Semitic)

I loved the BENEDICTION most **May God bless you and keep you and make His face shine upon you** two hours after sitting and standing and sitting and standing and stifling yawns and sleep and laughter too when the sounds of snores or farts interrupted the sermon **May God lift up His countenance upon you and give you peace** and handshaking and then we were out the door that was old and wooden and rotting because it was not a big church so not rich, and neither were we, no, we were poor but on Sundays we each got a candy bar at the little market on the long drive home because **In the name of the Father, and Son, and Holy Ghost** my mother's butt got tired too and so did her ears and maybe her heart though she wanted to believe in God, after all there had to be something better than five kids and no running water and a husband that sometimes called her the same cusswords he called his cows **Amen.**

2. Gold Foil

Each Sunday after a funeral of somebody we didn't know (we didn't know anybody in that church except the pastor and we didn't know him very well because it was a 30-mile drive from his house to ours and he made it only when my mother asked him, which was maybe once or twice, when she thought she was going insane, or when he thought we were hell-bent because we'd missed a month of Sundays) the church would be decorated with CHRYSANTHEMUMS left over from the wake

> **["wake n. 13. a watch or vigil by the body of a dead person before burial, sometimes accompanied by feasting or merrymaking;" a watch, it says, as if the body might rise up and speak, might confess finally its sins or condemn finally the sinners; merrymaking, it says, as if Lutherans ever the hell made merry]**

and the flowers would always be yellow, it seemed, and just beginning to fade, the tips drying up and going brown and curling inward like somebody in a coma closing like a flower closing for the last time, and I would stare at the mums in plastic pots wrapped in thin gold foil that tore if you barely touched it as I drank the blood of Christ **wine** and ate the body of Christ **bread** and I'd be glad that whoever died had not stuck around to see the flowers dying too, because they were sad there in their homely pots, sad and out of place in a church that was airless and dark, the only real sunlight coming through the face of Jesus in the altar's stained glass window so bright you couldn't look at it straight, only sideways, and even then it hurt your eyes.

3. Descending Into Sin

Worse than the old DREARY church was the new drearier basement of the pastor's house where we had confirmation class and where the windows were rectangles one foot high by two feet long that you couldn't crawl out of if there was a fire and they were basically useless anyway, those windows, because the pastor's wife who was very pretty and soft-spoken like wind loved plants and grew bushes and flowers and ferns around the whole house, blocking out the light completely so that the basement was pitch black when we first walked down into it, and I wonder now if the pastor wanted us to be afraid of **descending into darkness**, which was the phrase he always used to describe sin, though he was not as precise about sin as I would have liked, for example saying that getting remarried after a divorce wasn't a sin if the divorce was because the spouse was crazy, like his first wife who was, he said, crazy as a loon and maybe she was because he put her in a nuthouse and divorced her and then remarried the pretty wind-voiced lady who loved plants and adopted a child from Korea and named her my name, Debra, because she thought it was a nice and simple name and once she caught me in the bathroom singing **where have all the flowers gone** and she cried because it was the early seventies, after all, and there was a war going on and things were different then.

4. Brother Paul could've used some therapy

In the beginning our pastor only preached about life, you know: drugs and sex and rock 'n' roll and how Jesus would have fit right in with the Haight-Ashbury crowd because they were all fucked up looking for something better and that's what Jesus was dealing in those days—something better, his brand of dope—so of course there were all these Jesus freaks too, not just regular hippies, hanging around like some big party going on in the temple, and there's Jesus turning water into wine, or as the case coulda/woulda/shoulda been, Coca-Cola into LSD, and everybody tripping and seeing God, which is not what the pastor preached, not exactly, well not at all, no, rather he preached about everything that was going on now ("now" being 30 years ago—Jesus, has it really been that long?) and there wasn't anything anyone could do to change that fact, though they tried by demanding the pastor quit talking about life and instead preach straight from the Bible, especially from Paul's EPISTLES because, they said, Paul was so [self-]righteous and full of love, they said [come *on!* Paul was mad as hell at the Romans for putting him in prison, and he sure as hell didn't think much of women or, come to think of it, most of humanity if you read closely, which most people don't because they just don't read, don't know how to read, at least read what the words are really saying, not just what they *mean,* for chrissake], or other stories from the New Testament so they all could sleep better during the sermon and not have to pay such close attention to things that made them think hard because it gave them a headache and subsequently ruined their Sunday dinner of whole chickens and mashed potatoes with gravy and green beans and corn on the cob and homemade buttery rolls and apple pie with ice cream which is why so many were grossly overweight, whereas every Sunday we ate bologna and cheese sandwiches and Doritos because store-bought food was a treat after living on nothing but fresh beef and vegetables, so we liked it just fine.

5. Everything has a fragrance

What does God smell like? is what I wanted to know but was too afraid to ask my obvious question, obvious because I was a country girl and in the country everything has a scent: cow patties, grass, pond water, rain...everything smelling fine and full, and to smell a world like that you have to take it inside your mouth—talk about communion!—inside your lungs, inside your blood even, especially spring mornings right after the fruit trees blossomed a FRAGRANCE so thick and vast it could choke a lesser soul who'd never think to ask, **What does God smell like?** what we'd wonder sitting in the pews that were old and scent-darkened by lemon oil and hands that gripped the wooden backs to keep from swaying or falling, and the hymnals were old too, so the pages yellow and turning to dust though you couldn't see the dust yet but its scent was already rising from the thin paper under the black-ink notes rising to impossible heights, beyond the voice's range, like God was up there sitting at high C in a heaven you'd never reach and, damn, it hurt to try, vocal chords straining, the way I'd strain my nose to smell God in the motes of dust floating in a rail of light streaming through the glowing face of Jesus, thinking God'd be there first—in the smallest things I could see—or else not at all because everything starts from the bottom up, as every country girl knows, but the motes and light were always too high to stick my nose into, because I didn't know yet that even the darkness, the skin, the voice is full of dust.

6. Jesus as teen idol

The boys who went to church weren't better than the boys who didn't, they were just more scared of being bad, but not all of them because a few were bad whenever and wherever they pleased including in church, like this boy whose name I can't remember except that it didn't suit him, was a homely name and he was already handsome at ten and would be, you could tell, handsomer as he got older (though he never got much older, moving to another state and drowning in a lake after he dived off a pontoon and struck his head on a tree trunk floating beneath the water's surface just out of view), handsome in his bones, in his hands when he GROPED me in the church basement where we'd gone on an errand together to get some construction paper for a silly art project that had nothing to do with sanctity and everything to do with keeping a pack of ten-year-olds entertained until their parents came and took them home—a thank-God salvation for the Sunday school teacher—and kissed me too, my first kiss, under a poster of Jesus sitting on a rock with a little girl on his lap who looked a lot like me which, combined with that dead boy's kiss, is probably why for a long time, in fact through all my teen years, I had a crush on Jesus.

Fist

—in memory of Anita Vogel-Hyde

I no longer know the *names* of SIMPLE THINGS:

What turns the bread
brown and hard.

What makes the lamp
light up.

What you touch to
open a drawer.

It is this last THING that disturbs me most—its missing *name*—for it is what I see more than other THINGS. My eyes bad and the sickness pressing me brutally into my pee-stained sheets.

It will be the last THING I see:

and it is nothing.
NO THING.
Less than nothing without its *name*. So:

and I can't even *name* my HAND folded into a ball.

SIMPLE THINGS
SIMPLE THINGS
SIMPLE THINGS

Dying is not difficult. No. It's the world growing *name*-less and thus vanishing before my failing eyes.

The way she vanished.

she
she
she

I can't remember her *name*. The woman who loved me.

But I remember her HANDS. How lovely! The way they reached for THINGS as if through water. Their coolness on my brow when fever came.

What was her *name*?

Where did she go?

she said she'd come back

I will come back soon
I will see you again
we will go for a walk
you and I we'll

Haunted

This is where
you find them.

HERE.

At the end of the blue-slate road that disappears into timber so dense it's just a black scab on the lip of the world.

CREOSOTE CAVERN.

Watch out!

Bears wake inside.

SHE SAID ONCE SHE AND HE WENT THERE AND WAITED ALL NIGHT FOR A GLIMPSE, A SIGN. IT WOULD BE LIKE SEEING GOD, SHE SAID. OR MAYBE JUST THE VIRGIN MARY.

(She wasn't Catholic.)

NOTHING HAPPENED. IT WAS A PRETTY NIGHT. SHE HUMMED WITHOUT THINKING, MUSIC FILLING HER HEAD ALONGSIDE THE WHIPPOORWILL SONGS—MEANT IT WAS GOING TO RAIN.

(Not her humming. Whippoorwill songs.)

AFTER ALL THE CIGARETTES WERE SMOKED AND THE WHISKEY DRUNK, THEY GOT UP TO LEAVE. COULDN'T FIND HIS TRUCK. LOST IN THE WOODS FOR OVER AN HOUR. AND SOMEWHERE INSIDE THAT HOUR A SCREAM SO FULL OF BILE SHE WANTED TO DIE RIGHT THEN AND THERE SO AS NOT TO HAVE TO HEAR IT AGAIN.

SHE LIVED. HEARD IT AGAIN. AND AGAIN.

SHE PEED HER PANTS.

TOLD HER MAN IT WAS THE WHISKEY MADE HER LOSE CONTROL.

SAID: "I AIN'T AFEARED A NOTHIN SO'S DON'T YOU FORGET IT, BABY."

Oh, my, well, there haven't been any bears in Missouri for years. Decades, even. Don't know where they all went, but they did. Why, I remember when I was a child there used to be bears everywhere. Hardly a day went by we didn't see five or six of them lumbering through the timber.

All right, yes, maybe that is somewhat of an exaggeration.

Excuse me, but what do you mean by timber?
I mean trees. Lots of 'em.
Like a forest?
Like a timber. You from the city, ain't you.

IN YOUR NECK OF THE WOODS

Sun is hot. Air is still. Cicadas singing their metal death rasp.

He presses the turkey's neck to the ground, presses a broom handle over the neck, steps on the broom handle, grabs hold of the turkey's head and yanks. Head rips free.

Turkey body flapping.

He looks at the wattle. It's red. He never noticed how red before today. Red like it doesn't belong in the world.

His stomach turns.

He tosses the head to the cats waiting by the fence and understands with startling finality he is going to die. Not today. But soon enough. He'll be a ghost haunting the woods.

Or he'll be nothing.

If you didn't know what a tree was you'd think there were giants swaying in the dark.

You'd think the night was haunted.

You'd think: *At least I am not alone.*

AND THEN HE'LL LOOK RIGHT THROUGH YOU, YOU DON'T EXIST, YOU'RE FORGOTTEN. AND HE'LL BE BACK TO WHERE HE WAS FORTY YEARS AGO, THIRTY, TEN, LAST WEEK. AS IF HE CAN'T HELP IT. AS IF WARM HANDS ARE FOLDING AROUND HIS BALLS, KNEADING, AND THE DESIRE FILLS HIM WITH SUCH DISGUST HE CAN'T STAY AWAY. JUST TO SEE THEM ONE MORE TIME. RIGHT THROUGH YOU. HAUNTED, HE IS, AS THE WOODS.

— Gimme a cigarette, will you?
— I just got only one left.
— Guess it should be yours, then.
— We can share it.
— Hey, that's all right, thanks.

— Think we'll see 'em?
— I hope so. But I hope not, too. Know what I mean?
— I do. Yes, I do.

— It's nice out here. The dark's nice. Cool.
— Stars are pretty.
— I could die out here and it'd be okay. I think.
— It's just the screaming before you die that's bad.
— I wouldn't scream.
— Bet you would. Bet you'd scream your damn head off.

HIS IDEA OF GOD:

Bear gnawing on a cow bone. Trying to get at the marrow.

— What you mean you don't know which way's the truck?
— I mean I don't know, that's what.
— Shit.

— I think it's that way.
— We just come from that way, shithead.
— No we didn't, we came from that way.
— No we didn't cause there's a big oak I ain't seen before.
— Shit. You can't tell the difference between one tree and another.
— Sure I can.
— Bullshit.
— I can.
— Okay then, what's that there?
— Oak tree.
— And that?
— Oak tree.
— It's a maple.
— Ha ha no it ain't.
— Yes it sure as hell is.
— No it ain't, look at the leaves. They ain't the same as the oak.
— It's a pin oak, that's why.
— You're makin that up.
— Nope I ain't, I…

— Jesus fuckin' Crisco what the hell was that?

Bears wake inside.

Then again, it's not so much dying that scares him but dying alone. Though you'd think he'd be used to it by now. Alone all these years. Nary a friend. People never liked him much. Found him too opinionated. Nothing wrong with having opinions—long as you keep them to yourself.

He can hear the crunching of cats chewing on turkey bones. Finds comfort in it. The way things ought to be. Death giving life giving death. And so on and so forth. He'd like to be there somewhere in the middle. Not too obvious, only an irreplaceable part of things. Like this day. The sun rolling over the tree line so fat he can almost hear its fiery roar.

The day seems bigger than him. Swallows him like a gnat.

It's true: Even the gnats seem to have a bigger place in the day.

Move like smoke they do, she says, spits chaw.

Sharp they are, all skinny-tooth and blade. Uh-huh.

Yup. That's right.

SPITS.

SCRATCHES.

LOOKS.

Nothing.

Said:

THEY'S THE OLD MAN'S TIMBER. HE COULD MAKE SOME MONEY SELLING OFF A FEW A THOSE WALNUTS. SHIT. SOME MONEY. SMALL FORTUNE THERE HE'S GOT BUT HE WON'T DO IT. NO. SOME DAY HE'S GONNA DIE IN THE HEART A THOSE TREES AND SOME BEAR'S GONNA CHEW HIS OL' BONES TO DUST AND HE'LL JUST BE GONE.

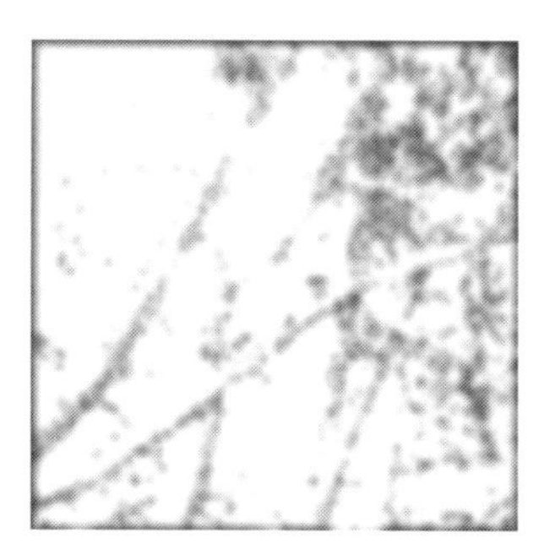

He can hear them from where he stands at the end of the blue-slate road. Hear them all. All the voices now and then and maybe somewhere in the future, too. Time yet to come. This deep in the woods so hard to tell which direction death moves.

AND SHE WILL DREDGE THE SCREAM FOR
THE REST OF HER LIFE AND STILL DENY IT.

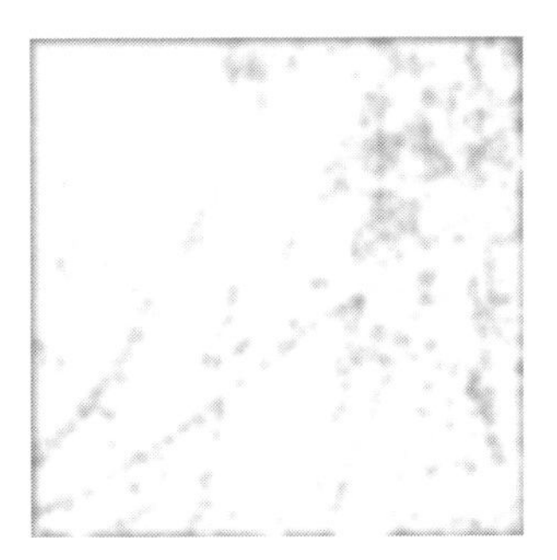

Whose idea of god now?
Bears wake eternal in your red-wattle heart.

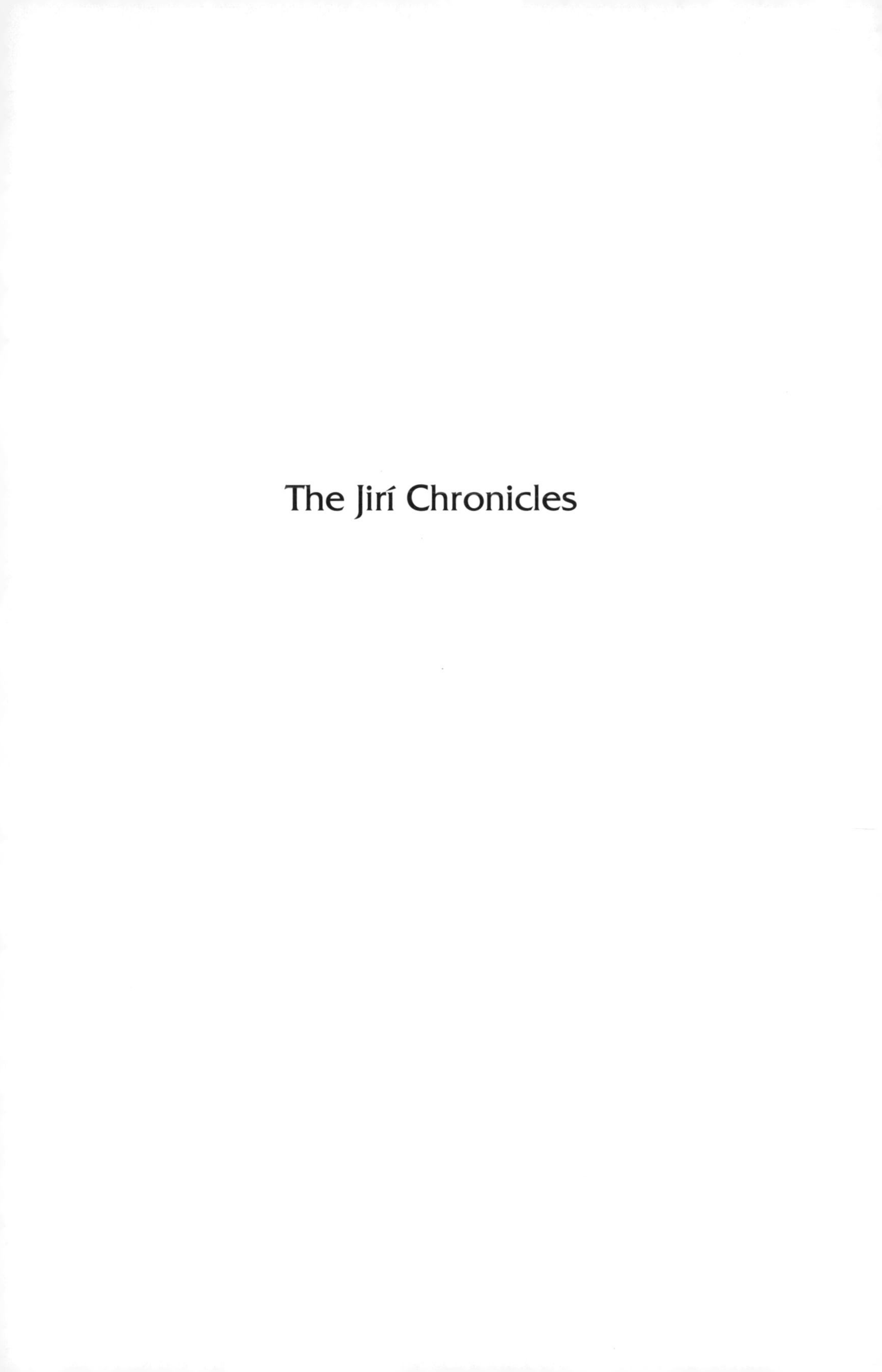

The Jirí Chronicles

the real Jirí Cêch™

Face it:

150 years of history and romance won't help you get laid.

Let me teach you the fine art of exaggerating your sex life.

*Offer does not include physical, aural, psychic, or other personal contact with the author, her family, friends, including but not limited to imaginary, business associates, coworkers, pets, plants, including but not limited to those growing in the wilds of her back and/or front yard and/or trunk of her automobile, new or used, or any of author's personal and/or impersonal possessions, including but not limited to those acquired at a future date, such as replacement vacuum cleaner bags or laundry detergent, with or without bleach, said items thereby falling under the ownership of said author who does not want some weird, awkward, icky, and possibly felonious contact with respondents who just don't get it due to inadequate education within a U.S. or foreign school system, in the former case most likely public and insufficiently funded by taxpayers unwilling to take responsibility for the society in which they so comfortably thrive, or due to individuals choosing a life of ignorance wherein literature and other art forms and intellectual pursuits are relegated to the region in said individuals' cerebrum containing "Things that make my brain hurt bad," like, quite possibly, this.

Respond now!
and I'll show you how to be a vampire or victim
—*your bloody choice!*

NO EXTRA CHARGE!

Czechoslovakian Rhapsody
Sung to the Accompaniment of Piano

A DEAD GERMAN

> **A dead German sat in front of his television set for five years** with the lights of his Christmas tree flashing beside him, and none of his neighbors noticed.
>
> "Someone said once that he had gone off to a home, I didn't ask any more," said Monika Majarres, who lived in the same Hamburg apartment building as Wolfgang Dircks, a divorced, disabled loner who died in 1993 at the age of 43.
>
> The landlords came knocking only after the bank account from which Dirck's rent and bills were automatically paid ran out.
>
> Next to the no-longer-functioning television set and the still twinkling tree, they found his skeleton with his TV listings magazine still on his lap and open to the page for Dec. 5, 1993.

You would say, "Serves him right, fucking German bastard," like a joke, but you'd mean it. Your arrogant Czech tongue spitting out the word *German* like a hair, hairball from the tongue of a cat, Bohemian dog, you. Should I be horrified that I slept with you *after* you insulted Jews, Germans & North American Indians? It was hot that night, and the bar was hot, and you were dressed in an undershirt and jeans and hot from playing soccer, hot so drinking cold Pilsner[1] of course, and you said, "You look hot tonight, woman," and flipped that big Czech hand of yours as if the w o r l d w o r l d w o r l d w o r l d w o r l d w o r l d w o r l d w o r l d w o r l d w o r l d were nothing more than gnats swarming/breeding, and you added: "At least all these horny bastards think so." Which was a lie; no one saw me come in. What you really meant was: *We would like to suggest that Paradise was never really lost. We would like you to consider that Eden is a state of mind, and that the mind of Adam and Eve (yes, they thought as one!) has not evolved beyond the ability to recall and thus conjure Paradise: its light and heat and scent. We would like to urge you to embrace the possibility of Heaven-on-Earth and* **come a little bit closer, you're my kind of [wo]man, and I'm all alone.**

---

[1] Pilsner is Czech beer: "'Czechs like to drink Czech beer because it's the best in the world,' said Antonin Jelínek, editor-in-chief of *Pivní kuryr*, a magazine for beer connoisseurs. 'They'd have to be pretty desperate to drink anything else.'" (Source: *The Prague Post*, page A8, Nov. 25-Dec. 1, 1998)

I came.

Closer.

PAIN: THIRSTY NO MORE

You're a vampire and when you suck me you suck me dry: There's nothing left but teeth marks, bruised to blue. I *want* you to go when you go. I *want* you to stumble over the diminutive pebble somewhere anywhere there just beyond my door—Goliath taken down by disregard—and fall and bruise black for you disregard me.

I said: *"It looks like the world turned inside out, like a part of the surface of the moon transplanted onto the surface of the sea."*

You said: *"What the hell are you talking about?"*

I said: *"Pain."*

You said: *"Oh."*

CZECHS WATCH LESS TELEVISION

Czechs eschew boob tube

Czechs watch less television than any group in Europe except German-speaking Swiss, according to a study released Nov. 19. The study, called Television-98, found Czechs average 130 minutes of daily viewing time compared to an average of 198 minutes per day for West European adults. Television-98 was conducted by the marketing firm IP in Düsseldorf, which is associated with the German commercial television channel RTL.

Hungarians, averaging 235 minutes daily, watched the most TV according to the study. German-speaking citizens of Switzerland averaged just 128 minutes a day.

On My Mother's Side I am part German, Jew and North American Indian. It was not that my mother's side of the family was unprejudiced, eager to achieve the hybrid vigor,[2] spawn a new race of superhumans who would somehow bring Peace, Tranquility and, yes, perhaps even *Joy to the World*. No, it was that the Jews lied about their Semitism, and the North American Indians lied about their "savage blood," and the Germans

---

2 Hybrid vigor: a term used in animal husbandry and horticulture to indicate the result of cross-breeding wherein only the sturdiest genes from each species are reproduced in offspring, the weaker genes having been supplanted by the genes most useful for survival.

who did not yet have the murder of six million Jews on their conscience lied about not knowing the difference between a Jew and an Irishman (*ref.* "Genealogy: Bad to the Bone," p. 92).

You of the Bohemian[3] blood would find my blood of English, Scotch and Welsh **On My Father's Side** somehow more palatable, as if a vampire like you had the luxury of being a bloody gourmet.

I *should* be horrified that I slept with you after you insulted Jews, Germans & North American Indians. Why am I not? Even now, at this late date, why does it occur to me as nothing stranger than, say:

COLD PRESSED VIRGINS

An open letter to Miloš Zeman

Dear Mr. Prime Minister:

In the Sept. 30–Oct. 6 issue of *The Prague Post*, it was reported that a large pig farm is operating on the site of the former concentration camp in Lety, near Písek.

In the Lety camp, innocent people — above all Sinti and Roma [Gypsy tribes] — experienced eternal suffering. They were tortured and tormented, left to die of hunger and worked to death.

On June 6, 1991, the European Union ratified a Convention of Security and Cooperation in Europe. It was signed by the member countries at that time. The convention also entailed the obligation to maintain memorials where crimes against humanity were committed during the Second World War.

It is my opinion that a pig farm on the territory of a former concentration camp is a severe offense against the provisions of the above-mentioned convention. It also violates all rules of good relations of the Czech state toward its national minorities.

I ask you, dear Mr. Prime Minister, to see to it that the pig farm is transferred to another location.

Simon Wiesenthal
Vienna

— The writer, who will be 90 on Dec. 31, spent four-and-a-half years in Nazi concentration camps during World War II, in which 89 of his relatives and family members were exterminated. He has crusaded against genocide ever since and calls himself a "deputy for the dead." Translated from German by Valerie and Alan Levy.

The citizens of the Missouri town where I grew up have filed a class-action lawsuit to shut down the newly built corporate pig farm because "its odor creates an environment making daily life unbearable." Question: Does the stink of the future out-rank the stink of the past? Must the task of living always consist of holding one's nose?

---

[3] You think I don't know that my calling you "Bohemian" is an insult to you, you Prague-lodyte, you who used "Bohemian" to disparage your own brother because he weeps the tears of a lover during—*o mein gott!*—Wagner's *Tristan und Isolde*. You think I don't know Germany occupied Bohemia during World War II, that your father who believed in the intellectual superiority of Bohemians—after all, he had let German soldiers win at chess in order to keep his shoe repair business open—your father, an otherwise good man, good father, told you repeatedly, rapping you on the head with his knuckles, that the fall of Bohemia was the fall of civilization. "From here on out," *knock knock* "it's facedown in the gutter and piss on your breath and don't you ever," *knock knock knock* "ever whisper Bohemia again because it is gone, you understand," *knock knock* "a memory, a dream, a cloud—vanished." You think I don't wonder if he wasn't right, damn him, watching the Germans come and go, the Soviets come and go, the Americans come and stay and sit in coffee houses reading Kafka and pretending to understand the meaning of *refugee* and *exile* and *irretrievable* while here at home refugees in exile mourn their irretrievable past beneath a billboard advertising underwear that costs more than their life savings. You think I don't know Bohemia was the world's most legendary enclave of refined pleasure and now it's gone. *Kaput!* as Hitler grinned, watching the ash of Kafka's sisters fall upon the sill of the window of his bastard dream.

IN THE WINTER OF 1942 IT WAS COLD IN LETY. THE WOMEN LAY PRESSED TOGETHER IN THE HARD WOODEN BUNKS. SOME WERE VIRGINS. THEY DIED WITHOUT KNOWING THE PLEASURE OF HAVING A MAN INSIDE THEM.

CZECHOSLOVAKIAN RHAPSODY

I had you inside me. It was a pleasure. I should be horrified.

CO JE TO PTAKOPYSK?[4]

In the hot bar the British tourist at the next table said, "The South Devon[5] tourist board seized upon any clue, however slight, that tied Christie[6] to the region." This has nothing to do with anything except that as a writer I am always eavesdropping on conversations, especially when they are more interesting than the one in which I'm engaged.

You said:	*"You really liked those Injuns, eh?"*
I said:	*"North American Indians."*
You said:	*"Injuns. Savages. Red niggers."*
I said:	*"You are joking, aren't you?"*
You said:	*"Of course I'm joking. Don't be silly."*
I said:	*"My great grandmother was an Indian."*
You said:	*"What the hell is a platypus, and how come I've never tasted one?"*

The British tourist sighed, "It's a mystery."

A COMPLETE COURSE FOR BEGINNERS

Jedl ptakopysk.	He was eating platypus.
Snédle ptakopysk.	He ate the platypus.
Jedle.	He was eating.
Najedl se.	He had something to eat.
Najedle se ptakopyskem.	He ate his fill of platypus.

---

4 Czech for: *What is a platypus?*

5 This is the name of my elder brother, in fact derived from Devon, England, where my father (who was a flight engineer in 30 bombing missions over Germany) was stationed during World War II.

6 Dame Agatha Christie, the British mystery writer.

THE (W)HOLE OF MY INVENTIVENESS

I was walking along a slope so steep and high it was impossible to see what lay below, obscured by the fog of ignorance only dreams and faulty imagination can provide, and I saw a boulder made of brown clay compacted by time, exposed now to the elements, and I knew the moment I set foot upon its slippery-damp surface it would crumble and I'd go toppling down into the w HOLE of my inventiveness, yet set foot upon the boulder anyway, and it did crumble, and you twitched in your sleep, softly crying, "Fuck!" and woke me.

I was saved.

You continued sleeping, snoring, victim of apnea.[7]

I think we knew each other centuries ago, were ill-fated lovers. We do not know each other now. Though we are ill-fated nonetheless.

> xenophobia: hatred of foreigners
> [xenos = stranger (Greek) + phobos = fear (Greek)]
> [[xenophobia really = fear (therefore hatred since we hate what causes us fear because fear is a loathsome human characteristic, thus we first hate our self then loathe our self then hate the stranger whom we fear) of strangers]]
> [[[don't argue with me, I know I'm right]]]

AUF WIEDERSEHEN

Some say it is the wise alone who seek
harmony in body, mind & spirit.
—Anonymous Ad Copywriter

I want you to go when you go. When you are gone I want you back.

---

[7] A sleep disorder in which the air passageway is blocked, causing night terrors and sometimes death. (I sat up in bed and watched you sleep and timed the silences between breaths. I imagined a silence that went on in perpetuity, imagined myself tucking the blankets under your big permanently silent chin, getting dressed, and calmly walking out of the hotel as if nothing had happened, as if I'd never known you.)

Why does my body play deaf to the protests of my mind? It's the plight of the vampire's victim, *ano?*[8] Teeth wounds on my thighs. Metal-bitter blood on my lips. This close to death and it's my murderer I cry out for. Boulders of clay, feet of clay, you're a clay-footed devil[9] and your father played chess with Nazis to save the soles of shoes while the souls of my ancestors cried, "Devil! Bloodletter!" and marched to the points of bayonettes to stand on the high steep slope with nowhere to step but upon the clay that crumbled forever into a future where their progeny sleeps with you who would wish all of them (and plenty others, too) dead once more in order to cleanse the world of the guilt you can neither bear nor name and thus wish yourself to disappear, vanish into the night: bat-winged wolf-howl mist and not a human scent for miles.

Each time I open this book[10] : : : : : : : *What is a platypus?*

Platypus: semi-aquatic egg-laying mammal, or monotreme (*Ornithorhynchus anatinus*). Also called duckbill, it has a rubbery, duckbill-shaped muzzle, no teeth, and no external ears. Its head, body, and tail are broad, flat, and covered with dark-brown fur; its feet are webbed. The adult male is about 6' 5" tall, handsome, well-endowed. The platypus eats small freshwater women of 1/2 German-Jew-North American Indian descent and originates from the Czech Republic—or what was once Bohemia, now vanished.

GENEALOGY: BAD TO THE BONE: PART I

My maternal grandmother died believing she was half German, half Irish. She was not. Here's the story:

Toward the end of the nineteenth century my great-grandfather, who was a Jew and whose last name began with the letter G, emigrated from Germany to the United States. This was his

8 *ano* = *yes* (Czech)
9 *cert* = devil, *dàbel* = devil, *jednohubka* = canapé
10 *Teach Yourself Czech: A Complete Course for Beginners* by David Short.

second emigration. The first was during the European Revolution, as an infant carried by his parents. There had been "some sort of trouble" and the G family had escaped it by fleeing to America. (Something about Kaiser Wilhelm. Something about money and/or property. Something vague but unseemly, perhaps dangerous but not, perhaps, noble.) The trouble vanished, or was momentarily forgotten by the Kaiser, and the G family returned home only to flee again for similarly vague but [perhaps] ignoble reasons. The family settled somewhere in the area of Beaver Dam, Wisconsin—that region known for its VAST Jewish-emigré population (ha ha ha!).

There were six children in the G family: three girls and three boys, one of whom was my great-grandfather. Something happened to the parents; either they again returned to Germany to face whatever political music was playing (Wagner?) or they died or they simply could not afford to feed, clothe, and shelter a brood of six. Therefore, the girls were sent to live with a family by the name of Johns, and the boys were sent to live with a family by the name of Clark. The Clarks were Irish. My great-grandfather took not only their name but their heritage, and passed it on to (1) his daughter (my grandmother) whom he never told otherwise, and (2) his son (my great-uncle) whom he told shortly before his death, shamefaced, though it was never clear whether his shame arose from the 70-year charade or his Jewishness. Let me explain:

My great-grandfather hated being a Jew. It shamed him. Whether it was the anti-Semitic climate in Germany or the anti-Semitic climate in Beaver Dam, or the anti-Semitic climate in his soul, my grandfather wanted so badly to fit into the world—a world that offered the possibility of rejection wherever he went—that he himself became anti-Semitic. He was a handsome man with olive skin and black hair and eyes, and a thick black mustache, and a streamlined soldierly physique. There was an exoticism about his appearance that couldn't be explained away (though he tried) by saying he was not only Irish but Black Irish: finer, rarer, worthier.

He was worthy to Hattie, my great-grandmother: a tall big-boned German woman, her blue eyes drawn to his black eyes like day to night. She knew his true identity for he confessed it one evening after they had kissed and kissed deeply, and she had hinted at their shared future by saying, "I vish to go on kissing you forever—if you know vhat I mean." Loved him especially for the burden of his self-hatred: the limping melancholia it lent him.

AND YOUR ARYAN EYE, BRIGHT BLUE[11]

Ah, yes! I remember you years ago, when you were in the shape of a young man with Aryan looks of blue eyes and blond hair, and an Aryan last name (von Something-or-other), and an Aryan hatred for JEWS and GYPSIES and BLACKS and HISPANICS and HOMOSEXUALS and anyone everyone all who did not appear Aryan, as I did then in my German-skin phase, my eyes-Swiss-blue phase, my English-tongue-and-cheek phase. And I remember, I remember that last night you visited me before I fled to Europe, you were hung over and disgusted because you had fucked a Jewish woman ("But she had blonde hair!" you cried.) and how you felt, you said, "unclean" and "damaged," and how those words toppled incongruously from your young ignorant lips, the way "genocide" and "supremacy" might spill from the lips of a three-year-old boy—for the implications of the words are as yet incomprehensible to him of the small dick the incomplete prick, and the words themselves only sounds his father makes when he's pissed and self-righteous and light-in-the-pocket after a long shitty day at the office. And I remember how I could not bring myself to declare, "My great-grandfather was a Jew," and how the shame of my reticence made me hate you that night so that when you said, "I love you," and kissed me good-bye I shuddered, and when you'd gone I scrubbed my lips with a rag until they bled.

I should have sent you the part-Jew-bloody rag with a note reading: "Fuck this, you fascist disease, you crime against humanity."

Instead, when I ran into you ten years later I kissed you on the cheek and asked about your health and your new wife. Who was Irish.

---

[11] From the poem "Daddy" by Sylvia Plath (b. 1932). She committed suicide in 1963 by sticking her head in an **OVEN** and turning on the **GAS**.

Which of these descriptions comes close to your view of our relationship?

A serious problem	46%
Not serious	32
An adversary	14
Undecided	8

Do you approve or disapprove of the way we are dealing with our attempt at love?

Approve	37%
Disapprove	37
Undecided	26

SOURCE: THE PEW RESEARCH CENTER. BASED ON PHONE INTERVIEWS CONDUCTED SEPT. 4-11

"WHAT YOU NEED IS A GOOD ETHNIC CLEANSING!"

...and I cried, I wept like a grandmother, *which I was: mother to half-breeds, grandmother to quarter-breeds, great-grandmother to eighth-breeds, and so on and so forth, my descendants fractionalized until there is so little of my blood left I could vanish with a paper cut.*

The English did not wipe out my tribe of agrarian pacifists, nor the French, nor the German. It was the Iroquois who loved to fight us for we were not them, and the Sioux who loved to breed us for we were beautiful, and my father who loved fire water more than good-for-nothing squaw daughters and so sold me to a wealthy farmer whose blood was as irrelevant as his skin red as mine when it was summer and the fields to be mowed. (All right, he was a white man—half German/half Swiss—but he bled red, and though he was more hirsute than the pigs he farmed, I let him between my pretty fawn thighs because he was a kind man, a big ugly kind man, a burnt-skinned kind man like a roasted pig, and I let him come (he came) because I saw the world to come and there was no place in it for me, the last of my breed.

Great-great-granddaughter who invents my words here, hear my inquiry: What do you get when you cross a stream with a horse?

Answer: You get to the other side, baby, that's all.

THIS IS NOT BOHEMIA:

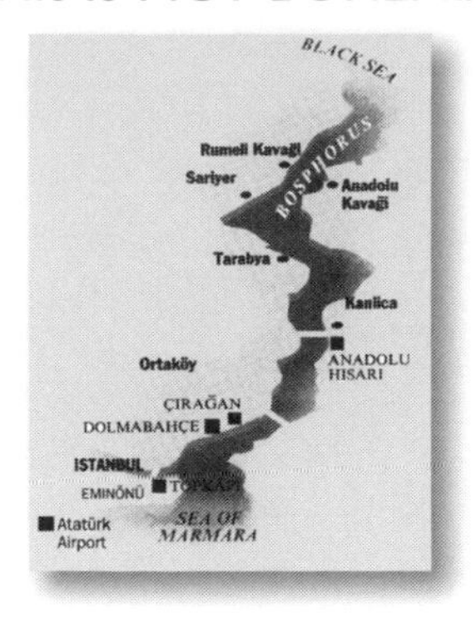

NOR IS THIS:

> *[Czech] history has taught them to keep their heads down, and to make an ironic comment or* **JOKE** .[12]

That hot night in a bar a North American Indian sat down at our table and told white man jokes and you told red man jokes, and the two of you laughed and laughed and laughed and laughed as if to say: "Look how far we've come, white man and red man, able to laugh at each other without one of us dying with a knife or bullet in our back!"

The jokes were not funny. I yawned and excused myself to the bathroom, and when I returned I sat down and asked: "What do you get when you cross a stream with a horse?"

And you of the white skin and he of the red skin grinned and shook your heads, and I paused a moment to build suspense, then answered: "A platypus."

ZNOVA: CO JE TO PTAKOPYSK?[13]

Platypus, *Ornithorhynchus anatinus cowboyishnus*
On each ankle the male platypus has a spur connected to poison glands in the thighs; these spurs are used against an attacker or against a woman who is one-half German/Jewish/North American Indian. The poison is not fatal to her but causes intense pain.

---

[12] Fodor's *Exploring Prague*. Emphasis on the word **JOKE** is mine.
[13] Again: *What is a platypus?*

It's not just that I'm half German/Jewish/North American Indian, is it. It's also that I'm a woman. And you would say with a predictability that would make meteorologists climax: "Oh, here we go with that fucking feminist piss-and-moan crap, pissing and moaning about injustice when what you're really pissed about is that you have a hole and I have a cock. Meaning, you represent absence. I represent the opposite."

(What is the opposite of absence? Is it you, here,[14] kneeling between my thighs like some reluctant communicant, waiting for a miracle you can no longer convincingly argue, no longer believe in? Or is the opposite of absence the memory of absence, for you are more present to me in my memory of your leaving—foot crunch upon gravel, *chît-chît* of lighter lit, scent of smoke fading.)

PAIN: CHILDREN SUPPLIED THE ART

You with whom I fell in love at first sight: you bloodsucking/bloodletting/bloodcurdling vanished-Bohemian vampire: you transplant to land of cowboys and *injuns*: you with guilt up your ass, spurs on your boots, ice in your heart: you cause me pain

I said:	*"Ouch."*
You said:	*"You want me to not thrust so deeply?"*
I said:	*"I want you to take off your boots."*
You said:	*"Fucking demanding mutt of a woman."*
I said:	*"The spurs, too, lover."*

for I should shudder at the memory of you inside me. Instead, I want to bear your children.[15]

---

[14] You're not here, of course; I'm writing this in my study miles and miles from where you are, and this is merely paper and ink. Lest there be any confusion with reality.

[15] Scientists recently identified the gene responsible for genocide. Here's how it works: When a member of a species or race (as in humans) meets another member of a species or race with qualities the former finds somehow reprehensible (such as wacky religious beliefs, flagrant ignorance, too shrewd money management skills, or even, ironically, bigotry) the genocide gene will compel the former individual to take measures to eliminate the latter individual. The most obvious methods are shooting, stabbing, gassing, burning, electrocuting, strangling, drowning, bombing.... Less obvious methods, but no less disagreeable, are rape (wherein the male deposits his seed in the reprehensible female, thus halving the strength of her →

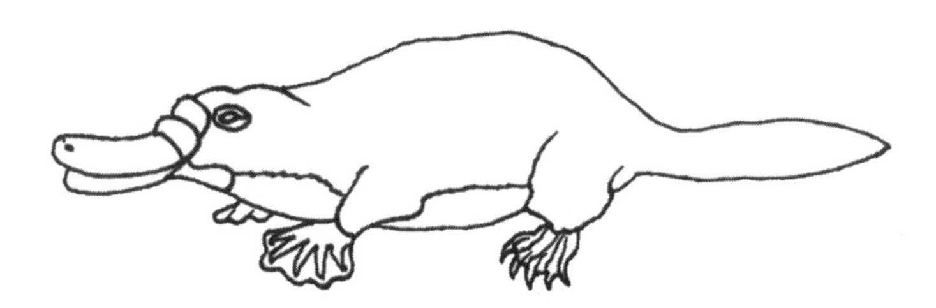

platypus

bloodline) or seduction (wherein the female seduces, then spends $200-$400 for the reprehensible male's seed in order to halve and thus reduce the strength of his bloodline). Unbeknownst to rapist or seductress, the genocide gene will default in these instances to produce a hybrid vigor, usually consisting of reprehensible traits of both individuals, thus "guaranteeing" the perpetuation of the species for at least one more generation. (You understand that it's possible I've made all of this up. You also understand—if you know anything at all about the Human Genome Project—that I may not have made it up. The point is: I want you to question what you think you know or don't know, what you believe or don't believe. In other words: I want you to consider that you don't know your ass from a hole in the ground.)

(Let's have nothing here but white space. Let's have nothing but a cool plane of white for our tired tired eyes, our weary weary mind. My mind is weary, isn't yours? And perhaps also your heart? It's strenuous, this acute caring, this heavy penitence, this thing writers and readers do. Oh yes, we're in this together, you and I. Didn't you know? For godsake, don't you know that *yet*?)

THE 50 MOST BEAUTIFUL GUYS ON EARTH . . .

"Are Czechs," you said, dabbing a napkin at the blood oozing from the corners of your mouth. "My semen will cost you $200. That's half the price of a wad purchased at a sperm bank."

"You're joking, right?"

"Don't you see?" you grinned. "Don't you understand? I'm giving you an incredible discount!"

YOU'LL WANT TO TAKE ONE HOME WITH YOU!

(IT'S RAINING NOW. IN THE STREET OUTSIDE THIS CAFE, ALL UMBRELLAS ARE BLACK EXCEPT ONE: BRIGHT BLUE. LOOK HOW IT STANDS OUT! SUCH A BRIGHT BRIGHT BLUE BLUE UMBRELLA! I STUDY THE CLOTHES OF THE MAN CARRYING IT IN ORDER TO DETERMINE THE CHARACTER FLAW THAT WOULD HAVE HIM CHOOSE A BRIGHT BLUE UMBRELLA OVER A TYPICAL BLACK ONE. THOUGH HE'S DRESSED SIMILAR TO OTHER MEN—BLACK TRENCHCOAT, GRAY TROUSERS, SHINY BLACK SHOES—THERE'S SOMETHING ABOUT HIM THAT'S DIFFERENT, SOMETHING NOT QUITE RIGHT, SOMETHING *QUESTIONABLE*. I KNOW IT.)

A recent spate of incidents involving organized skinhead actions has prompted the government to propose a plan to create a new police unit dedicated to curbing racist violence. But Interior Ministry officials are not in favor of the move.

"No unit against skinheads is planned," even though increased skinhead activity is a reality, asserted Jan Decker, spokesman for the Interior Ministry. "We are only going to strengthen the anti-extremist unit so that it will monitor the skinhead movement more effectively than before," he said. The police can't just act against citizens because they have short hair and dress like a skinhead, he added.

WILD. AND CRAZY.

No one will make excuses for you, not even me. However:

It's true that shortly after you arrived in the United States a popular television program called *Saturday Night Live* began. It was a funny show. People watched it late Saturday nights and they laughed. They laughed hard. One of the skits they laughed particularly hard at was "Two Wild and Crazy Guys." The two wild and crazy guys were played by Steve Martin and Dan Aykroyd. They were funny, funny, funny. They dressed in ugly polyester-looking clothes that were too tight and too colorful and too unfashionable to not be funny. They were always trying to pick up "some crazy American chicks." Those two wild and crazy guys, how stupid they were! Ha ha! How crass! Ha ha ha! How sleazy! Ha ha ha ha ha ha ha ha ha ha ha ha ha ha ha ha ha!

They were Czechs.

One only has to imagine the humiliation you suffered as a result: a relatively new Czech in a relatively new world with nothing but the cheap polyester shirt on your back. Anyway, it wasn't so much that your father played chess with Nazis—chess, unlike war, is only a game—but that when your Jewish neighbors (the ones with the two children you used to play "cowboys and injuns" with) were arrested and shipped off to Auschwitz[16] and you asked him, your father of the Bohemian blood, "Why?" he replied, "Because they were very bad people." And when you asked, "But what did they do?" your father smacked you hard across the back of your head.

It was the smack that made you wild. The smack that made you crazy. The smack that made you turn to me in bed that hot hot night and whisper, "Platypus.... How do you spell it?"

P - L - A - T - Y - P - U - S

ORNITHORHYNCHIDAE
Platypus Family

The platypus is an extraordinary animal in appearance but well adapted for its way of life. It was discovered in 1797 in Australia. When the first specimen arrived at London's Natural History Museum, scientists were so puzzled by it that they believed it to be a fake and tried to pry the duckbill off with scissors.

---

[16] It's true that you could not possibly have been born yet, but the fact that you tell this story as if it were fact must mean something, you clinging to a memory that never was. (Of the two neighbor children who were shipped off to Auschwitz, one was a little girl with long black hair, wavy and perpetually beribboned, round black eyes that made you think of aching things you could not yet comprehend. It could be said that you loved her with a love far wiser than any eight-year-old boy could summon. It could be said she was your wife, love of your life, just waiting for the both of you to grow up. Of course, she never grew up. The Nazis were so kind to let her stay seven forever—the age she remains for you in your imaginary memory of her. Though sometimes, you confess, you think you see her walking down the street of any American city, dressed in blue, hair cut short now out of respect for her seven-year-old ghost. "Once," you said, "I even thought you were her. The first time I saw you. But I can smell the German in your blood. I can taste it. I suspect, though cannot be sure, it resembles the flavor of platypus.")

THE WONDER OF YOU

"Or be more energetic and propel yourself," said the British tourist, irritated by the heat and his partner's daftness.

You and I, on the other hand, looked at our watches:

I thought:	*The word "injun" resulted from men too ignorant, too stupid to pronounce "indian." And the word "indian" resulted from white men so stupid they thought Newport Beach was East India. Men so stubborn they insisted on calling the natives "Indians" even after their mistake clearly had been brought to their attention.*
You thought:	*Life wasn't easy under Communism but at least it was predictable.*
I thought:	*The world's worst murderers are made up of boys who never got into art school, or didn't make the soccer team, or kissed a little girl with red hair who cried "Ew!" and wiped her cherry-red mouth hard with the back of her hand. They never outgrew their wormy grudges; their grudges outgrew them, became monstrous parasites gnawing their slimy way through humanity. Or what was left of it.*
You thought:	*I wonder how long she will take to achieve orgasm.*
I thought:	*In the 1960s television show* Hogan's Heroes, *all World War II German POW camp officers and soldiers are stupid, and all World War II Americans, French, and British POWs are smart. The POWs play with their German captors the way cats play with mice.*[17] *They learn the German weaknesses which are* **HYSTERICALLY** *funny (if you are American or French or British) and infinite—or at least plentiful enough to make it through six television seasons.*[18]
You thought:	*Fucking who cares if she achieves orgasm, anyway.*

[17] Cats play with mice with a cruelty that makes them nearly human.

[18] Hogan's Heroes trivia: Werner Klemperer, who played the POW camp's pompous asinine idiotic Colonel Klink, was the son of the **Jewish-German** conductor, Otto Klemperer. Robert Clary (neé Robert Widerman), who played the beret-donning "frenchie" Captain Louis LeBeau, was imprisoned in a **Nazi** concentration camp as a child.

The British tourist leaned toward his partner and said, "Did you know that if you reverse only a couple of DNA strands in a cat you'll get a human?"

I turned to him and grinned: "That doesn't say much for cats, does it?"

His flat-heart expression didn't waver as he downed the rest of his ale and stood and left.

You watched every inch of his departure, looking down your elegant Czech nose at his plump belly and woman's ass, and you said, "Fucking potato-eater."

"I think 'potato-eater' refers to the Irish," I said.

You flipped that big Czech hand of yours through the gnat-teeming world and said, "Same thing. Potato-eaters, tea-sippers, Kikes, Krauts, Ruskies, Japs, Gooks, Chinks, Camel-jockeys...."

"You forgot Injuns."

"Injuns. Come on, woman, let's go have sex."

84 DOWN: DUCKBILL

There is nothing fake about the platypus. We know that now. Now we know it exists: hybrid vigor of creatures that should never have fornicated—they had so little in common. (Why, my god, a duck and a beaver! What could they have talked about that hot hot night? What could they have seen in each other but the insult of their difference.) Yes, now we know the platypus is real and stubbornly alive. And what is a platypus, after all? What does it represent that its name is on everyone's lips, silent but noticeable as a drop of blood about to drip onto one's chin?

It's Sunday afternoon and I'm taking a break from writing "Czechoslovakian Rhapsody Sung to the Accompaniment of Piano," sprawled on the couch doing a crossword puzzle simultaneously though abstractly thinking about the pungent scent between your legs, and there it is:

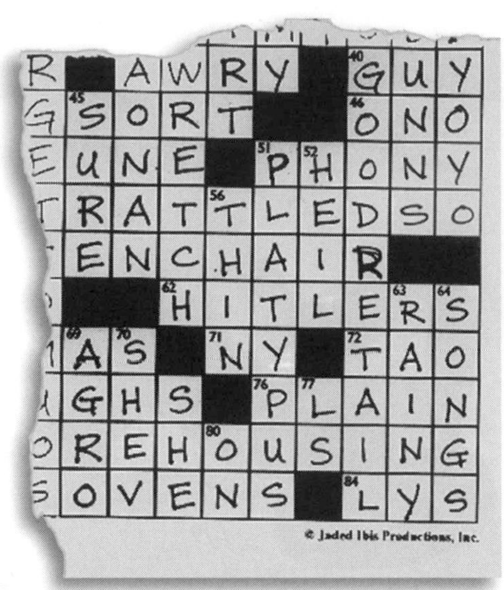

51 Down: Duckbill: an 8-letter word that begins with the letter **P.** I kid you not. Fucking **P-L-A-T-Y-P-U-S** is the answer. What are the odds! I put down the crossword puzzle[19] and close my eyes and think of you that last night when the heat of the wind and our scorched flesh created a vortex into which all histories light and dark good and bad left and right descended, and the world as we knew it (imperfect with its genocides and ethnic cleansings and [un]holy wars and racist swine) vanished like so many Bohemias—*kaput!*—and it was just you and me ***IMPROVED!*** and naked as in Paradise, getting ourselves back to the Garden, getting it on. And I thought that it just might be possible to forget about blood and skin and accents and finally feel the hot bending of each other's "sold-as-is" soul. Until you came inside me[20] and said breathlessly but matter-of-factly: "I knew you were good for *something*, woman."

BOHEMIA WAS

If you are ever in Prague and standing on the spot where Bohemia vanished forever and someone walks up to you and asks, *"Co je to ptakopysk?"* tell them the truth. Tell them:

A platypus is a creature that has outlived its time, has refused to evolve when everything around it was evolving into a more sensible form. It is archaic,

---

[19] Actual crossword puzzle not shown. Here's why: I requested from Tribune Media Services permission to use the lower right corner of a crossword puzzle from *The Kansas City Star* that I'd completed in ink, torn from the newspaper, scanned, and embedded in this story. Because the Trib could not tell me from which crossword puzzle the portion had been torn, they referred to it as "Crossword Puzzle" in their invoice. The invoice asked for $250, not for reprint permission, but only for the ***right to ask permission***. After my shameless begging, they reduced the amount to $150. Without actually stating, "Kiss my reproductive ass," I told them I would create my own puzzle. This footnote is my **REVENGE**.

[20] I.O.U. $200.

antediluvian, a breathing fossil, lone specter out of everyone's history wherein everyone, it seems, died at the hand of everyone else. Why? That is simply the nature of the platypus. Sleep with one if you wish. Feel the horror of its flesh inside your flesh, duckbill against your bloody lips, spurs against your blue-bruised thighs. If you can. If you cannot, then by all means succumb, succumb! You won't be alone.

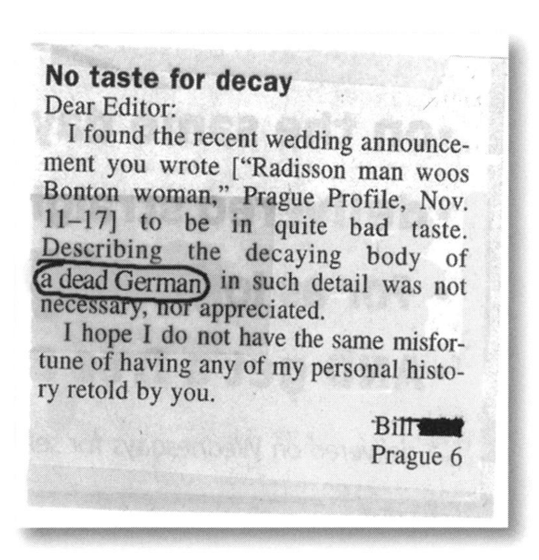

No taste for decay

Dear Editor:

I found the recent wedding announcement you wrote ["Radisson man woos Bonton woman," Prague Profile, Nov. 11–17] to be in quite bad taste. Describing the decaying body of a dead German in such detail was not necessary, nor appreciated.

I hope I do not have the same misfortune of having any of my personal history retold by you.

Bill
Prague 6

NOTE:

Platypuses are now protected by law and are quite common in some areas.

* All news clippings were appropriated from *The Prague Post*; some have been altered.

Life is scary.

All I could think of was carcinogens in bacon, burnt toast, water and air.... And then I began thinking of antibiotics: in dish soap, bath soap, Handiwipes…. Every time somebody used an antibacterial product, smaller weaker bacteria died, making room for bigger stronger bacteria. I thought it was just a matter of time till bacteria grew as big as Rottweilers. I thought that soon I'd be eaten by big growling slobbering streptococci. **AND THEN I KEPT THINKING.** Yes, thinking terrified me. And my fears grew every day until finally I couldn't get out of bed. I was paralyzed by the scariness of life. Then my doctor prescribed **CABLE TV**. He said it would make me stop thinking, said it would numb me to life's **BIG ISSUES**. Immediately I called **TIME WARMER CABLE**. The salesperson was so kind, so understanding. He said he received hundreds of calls a week from folks **JUST LIKE ME**, folks who couldn't stop thinking. And then he told me exactly what I needed to hear: **"CABLE TV WILL ABSOLUTELY CHANGE YOUR LIFE. I GUARANTEE IT!"** Well, I've had cable TV for a year now and haven't read a single book, newspaper or magazine, and I certainly haven't attended the theatre, symphony, opera, ballet or art museums. Even better, **I'M NOW CONVINCED I WILL NEVER DIE. HOORAY!!!**

Thank you, Time Warmer Cable!

especially when you don't have cable TV!

Life's not scary when you have cable TV

Glauke's Gown:
The Function of Myth

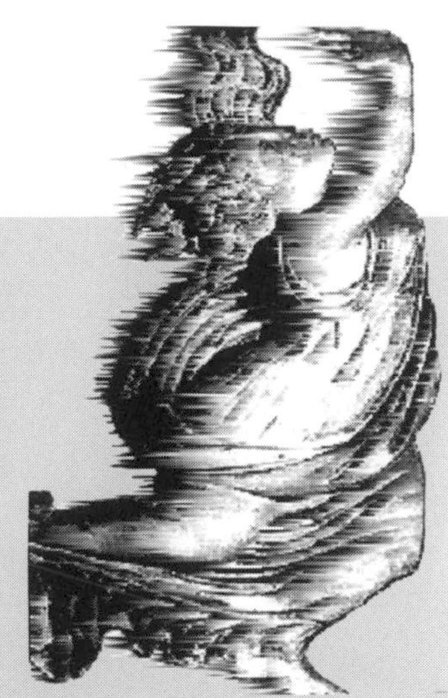

MEDEA
a synopsis

After taking the throne at Corinth, Jason the Argonaut, husband of Medea, fell head over heels for the pretty princess Glauke.[21] Medea, who had saved his ass on more than one occasion, became enraged with jealousy and sought revenge. But instead of "exacting revenge" on Jason, Medea aimed her sights on Glauke. She soaked a beautiful gown in a secret potion that "stored up the powers of fire" and sent it to Glauke. When Glauke tried on the gown[22] it burst into flames so hot they melted the flesh right off her bones. She threw herself into a fountain, but the water only made the flames burn hotter.

CHORUS: Medea, Medea, you bitch! No wonder it's your name on our lips.[23]

THE WOMAN turns to HER VERY BEST FRIEND seated next to her on her living room couch in front of a TV that's playing a video of *Lover*

---

[21] Yes, there are lots of names here, and if you know nothing of Greek mythology then it will be Greek to you. For the sake of clarity, say the role of Jason is played by Donald Trump, Glauke by Marla Maples, and Medea by Ivana Trump.

[22] What the hell was Glauke thinking!?! A gift from Medea, a woman who had dismembered her own brother in order to be with Jason?!? And what was Marla thinking!?! Signing a prenuptial agreement with The Donald that declared if the marriage didn't last five years she would get only $1-5 million of The Donald's $2 billion. How long did the marriage last? Almost five years. Big surprise. What were they all thinking, these women who love their men?!? Beautiful, yes. Wise…? Can't we blame it on environment, the inexorable way environment (i.e., the omnipotent media) molds young women into creatures who would do and say anything to get and keep their man. As a woman myself, I would like to blame it on environment, oh yes, for I am too ashamed to accept it as my "nature."

[23] This line appeared in Euripides' original version of his play, *Medea*. His editor forced him to delete it for fear of offending the mainstream reading public.

LOVER COME BACK
a synopsis

Doris is a scrupulous virginal advertising exec who wears silly hats, and Rock is an unscrupulous womanizing advertising exec pretending to be a shy rocket scientist who's never been laid so he can (1) get in Doris's pants and (2) distract her from pursuing a new ad account for a product that doesn't exist. Basically, Doris gets to wear a lot of white—and, of course, those silly hats—and Rock gets to wear a beard and tweeds when he's not barechested and perpetually tan. The sexual tension is palpable in their love scenes. What talented actors! Considering that in real life Rock was gay and Doris was married 4 times.

Come Back, starring Doris Day and Rock Hudson.[24] THE WOMAN and HER VERY BEST FRIEND are drinking Diet Cokes and eating salad and watching the scene where Doris realizes she's been duped by Rock and therefore gets mad, real mad, as mad as Doris can get.

"By the by," THE WOMAN says to HER VERY BEST FRIEND, "you will never ever believe what I did last night!"

HER VERY BEST FRIEND leans eagerly forward, salivating almost, almost twitching with un-Doris-Day-like anticipation. "What what what did you do?"

"Well," says THE WOMAN, cautiously glancing over each shoulder, first her right, then her left, though she's sitting in her own apartment where she lives alone, while on the TV screen Doris convinces Rock to strip down naked on a beach and then leaves him stranded there, taking his clothes with her, while THE WOMAN's mouth expands in a grin tinged with evil: green sky predicting hail, "I called Jirí every hour on the hour and hung up without saying a word."

"And then what?" asks HER VERY BEST FRIEND, drool gathering in her cleft chin.

"Then what *what*?" THE WOMAN asks.

---

[24] **BY THE BY:** Doris Day would never ever harm another living soul. I am not the only one who knows this. When I was a child my mother resembled a brunette Doris Day and everyone therefore believed my mother incapable of malevolent behavior. Even my mother believed this when she looked in the mirror and smiled at herself like Doris Day smiling at Doris Day. My mother's thought of spanking the piss out of me for drawing on the living room wall with broken crayons in shades of red melted to the mantra, "I am Doris Day, benevolent humanitarian, a phrase which may in fact be redundant, I don't know, whatever, anyway, I would never ever harm another living soul, not even my spoiled brat of a daughter." Yes, it's true: Doris made my mother a better human being and she saved my ass.

"What else did you do?"

"Why, nothing else!" Normally, THE WOMAN would never ever begin a sentence with "Why,...!" but she has been watching Doris Day for approximately 57 minutes, and Doris Day has gotten under her skin, transformed THE WOMAN into a woman whose language resembles Doris Day's language, not only in its vocabulary but its timbre: that sexy-but-celibate breathiness that is Doris, all Doris, why yes, Doris!

"Like I said," THE WOMAN continues, "I called him on the phone about a hundred times and then hung up!"

HER VERY BEST FRIEND recoils—not from horror but from an exquisite boredom, tangible and pungent and weighted as if Death himself [*Why is Death always a man, Nature always a woman?*] had just settled a wet mink coat around her shoulders.

PLEASE NOTE:

Days later at a cafe, a tomato seed[25] clings to HER VERY BEST FRIEND's napkin. She picks at it until it comes off under her fingernail. She must dig it out with another fingernail. She brings it to her face and studies it, thinking it resembles some object from inside the body: vile, best kept hidden. She shudders. Wipes the tomato seed under the table's edge.[26]

25 ***SHAMELESS SELF-PROMOTION *** See sections 9 and 11 of "Say What You Like" in my first book *Drought & Say What You Like*, winner of the Thorpe Menn Book Award.

26 Days later a child will run her little fingers under this very same table's edge and discover the tomato seed and pick it off with her tiny fingernail and stare at it long and hard. Then she will hold the seed toward her divorced-and-now-a-weekend-father father and exclaim, "Look, Daddy! A booger!" Daddy will glance around the cafe to see if anyone has heard his daughter's vulgar cry of delight, then brusquely clean the "booger" from her tiny finger with his paper napkin, then slap her hand hard and hiss, "Don't pick your nose, do you hear me?" And she will somberly nod her little head—though she will not be able to make the connection between the table's booger and her nose—and will rub her stinging little hand and start to cry until she remembers she is also not supposed to cry. When she grows up, she will become the Chief Financial Officer of a Fortune 500 company and date far younger men and be disparagingly referred to as "Big Bad Ball Buster" by males of equal or lesser corporate rank.

"Wasn't that just awful of me?" asks...no, *pleads* THE WOMAN. Awkward demanding plea couched in Doris Day vernacular. Doubtful and hopeful all at once.

"Yeah," HER VERY BEST FRIEND mumbles unconvincingly. "Awful."

Desperate to be bad, very bad, bad to the bone, THE WOMAN says: "It's probably a crime. A misdemeanor, at the very least. Harassment. I'm sure I could get arrested for it."

"Right," says HER VERY BEST FRIEND. Her eyes roll to the ceiling then stare at Doris Day singing on the TV screen, waist impossibly skinny below her impossibly pointy breasts below her impossibly golden hair, and quite suddenly she turns to THE WOMAN and asks, "Are you gonna eat the rest of your salad, or what?"

THE ART OF GETTING BUMPED

In ancient legends the combustible cloak[27]
was a weapon for exacting revenge.
—*Archaeology Magazine,* March/April 1997

There is nothing "exact" about revenge. As a science, it's not. As an art, it's possible. After all, it's the creativity of revenge that makes it worthwhile. Originality of the act. Brilliance: Medea also murdered her children so that Jason would have no heirs.

FIRST SON: Oh, what can I do? How can I escape my mother's hand? Where can I hide?

SECOND SON: I don't know. Dear brother, we are lost!

Lost like the screams of children disappearing into water or smoke.

27 Also known as *tunica molesta.*

SUSAN SMITH.[28] DEBORA GREEN.[29]

I had never felt so lonely and so sad in my entire life. I was in love with someone very much, but he didn't love me and never would. I had a very difficult time accepting that.... I dropped to the lowest point when I allowed my children to go down that ramp into the water without me.... My children, Michael and Alex, are with our Heavenly Father now, and I know that they will never be hurt again. As a mom, that means more than words could ever say.... My children deserve to have the best, and now they will.

—from the confession of Susan Smith

I'm sorry my children are dead.... Maybe God wanted me to be here to teach or tell me something. I cannot believe this is His plan for the rest of my life.

—from a letter written by Debora Green in the
Topeka, Kansas Correctional Facility

GAZING AT THE WORLD'S NAVEL...

we discover lint.

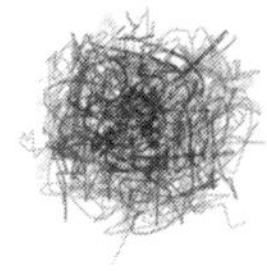

The human genome is a pigsty, bulging with non-genes, ex-genes, freeloader genes, viral detritus, pocket lint and chewing gum. All but a few percent of it appears to be doing nothing at all.[30]

```
Date: Mon, 25 Mar 2002  3:04:02-0500
To: prettygrl@bohemia.cz
From: jiricech@earthlink.net
Subject: Ontological concerns

Dear You:
God created heaven and earth, and somewhere in
```

---

[28] Depressed over her bad marriage and bad love affair, Smith drove to a lake, put her car into neutral, stepped out, released the parking brake, and let the car roll into water with her two sons strapped inside.

[29] Depressed after her husband had an affair, Dr. Green set her big house on fire. Two of her three children did not escape the flames.

[30] *Source:* Natalie Angier, for *The New York Times* online, June 26, 2000.

between a Man and a Woman rose up out of the dust and recognized in the other not so much the means by which desire could be met but the end of loneliness. They must have connected in that first encounter, Man and Woman, must have seen in the other the image of who they were inside their own mind--Narcissus and his reflection, perhaps?--otherwise it would have ended there: no more dancing toward each other, dancing around each other, dancing inside each other, trying to get a scent on the shape of "companionship."

I tell you it smelled like the shape of a piano about to fall on my head.

love,
Jirí Cêch

PICTURING THE PAST

Quiz

(1) Do you keep the promises you make to yourself?
No.
(2) Then how can you keep your promises to me?
Because I value you more than myself.

THE WOMAN cannot get the image of HER VERY BEST FRIEND's bored face out of her mind—though the TV is on and there's a war in Eastern Europe and people she has never met, now will never meet, *never ever,* are dying, will be dead in a matter of weeks days hours minutes seconds, are already dead, rotting even, mere flashes in the history of humankind (unkind humans!)—though she picks up the remote and turns up the volume and hears nothing—though somewhere, *out there,* indeed in a million neglected places, lives are coming to a horrible and tragic end—though all this and so much more, the face of HER VERY BEST FRIEND nevertheless stares back at her—*O how exquisitely bored!*—and she can think of absolutely nothing worse in the whole wide world.

(I gotta tell ya: I am *annoyed* by THE WOMAN, her shallowness, her self-absorption, her smallness. I've been her more times than I care to confess. Therefore I would like to eradicate her—well, maybe not *her* as *entity* (after all she's just invention, necessary configuration in a work of fiction that is about more and less than what it appears to be about), but rather her as *personality trait* (i.e., seriously flawed).)

(And isn't even this process of writing fiction[31] the ultimate act of conceit: *I think I know something important.* Tell me: What is more important than those distant deaths occurring now now now now now now now now now now now now now...?)

> **Then again if I don't say it,** thought Euripides, poised over parchment that was already taking on the distinctive scent of mold, **who in hell will?**

The gears in THE WOMAN's brain turn and grind and chew on the past, over the unhappy face of boredom, into the calm blank-slate-of-a-future where possibilities for revenge are bountiful and sweet! She turns off the TV and sits for a moment in the silent dark. She begins singing, quietly: "Euripides doo-dah, Euripides day! My oh my what a wonderful day!"

THE THRILL OF DISCOVERY

```
Date: Thu, 28 Mar 2002  17:01:24 -0500
To: prettygrl@bohemia.cz
From: jiricech@earthlink.net
Subject: Mythology

Dear You:
Everyone thinks the dragon is a mythical beast, but
I have proof of its existence. This particular dragon
claims she's in love with me but what a strange way
```

[31] Substitute: poetry, drama, personal essay, screenplay, etc.

```
she has of proving it. Every morning there's dog shit
on my doorstep. Fresh dog shit! I don't know where
she gets all of it; she doesn't even have a dog. But
there it is, practically steaming it's so fresh.
Sorry you had to hear this. :-(
Still, I thought you should know. :-)

love,
Jirí
```

Revenge is wicked and unchristian and in every way unbecoming... (But it is powerful sweet, anyway.)
—Mark Twain

Dear Mr. Twain:
Why is revenge sweet? I think it is bitter bitter bitter. The dried-blood taste it leaves in your mouth between your teeth remains far too long. Like Limburger cheese. Like literally kissing someone's ass.[32]

MEDEA: Let no one think of me as weak, the object of their simpering pity or contempt...

But, Medea! *Sweetheart!* Don't you get it? Don't you understand that the mere act of revenge is a confession to having been somehow wounded: betrayed, insulted, humiliated, shamed. And not only have you been wounded, you've stooped to advertise your wounds, for revenge lets THE *[black]* ~~WHOLE~~ *[in the]* ~~WIDE~~ WORLD know your pain, therefore confirming what you already suspect: *You're not worth your salt, baby.*

So the asshole left you for a younger more beautiful woman, so what? It's not about you, it's about him: His need for power and acceptance, more hair, bigger pecs, a thicker longer harder dick.

---

[32] Okay, I've never literally kissed anyone's ass, though I have pressed my lips to a lot of other things, including Limburger cheese. My ability to relate Limburger cheese with someone's anus is the result of **IMAGINATION!** The point being, I suppose: The best revenge takes imagination.

Take my advice: The best revenge is to lick your wounds in private—or find another lover and lick him. In public always pretend that it's not blood you're trailing behind you but an extraordinarily passionate and somehow corporeal...*aura!* That, or learn to write fiction wherein you can exact your revenge sweetly while simultaneously claiming to improve humanity.

5. Please read the following passage for comprehension:

> A certain Czech director whom I met at a certain film festival said he once asked his wife (a certain Czech actress whose name begins with the letter D) what she would do if he ever had an affair. D replied, "I'd kill her." The director cried, "Why her? Why not me?" And D pinched his scruffy cheek and cooed, "I could never kill you, darling, you're my husband!"

HOW FAST ARE YOU GOING?

Date: Mon, 01 Apr 2002 10:41:55 -0600
To: prettygrl@bohemia.cz
From: jiricech@earthlink.net
Subject: Here and There

Dear You:
Now you can go from lost to found at the speed of light. The way we find each other here in virtual space, our virtual love for one another. Let's never meet. Let's never learn each other's gestures, the way you might push your red (blonde? black?) hair behind your ears over and over again and again until I want to scream, break your wrist, wait until you have fallen asleep some fog-ridden night and take the blue-handled scissors and cut off your beautiful but unruly red/blonde/black hair. Trust me now: I don't want to know the smell of your morning breath, unwashed crotch, stale farts & belches. From this

remarkably clean distance even your anus smells like fresh-bloomed lilacs, or cinnamon sticks in coffee, or the breezes of my youth in Bohemia forever vanished beneath the smoke and dirt of culture, or lack of culture.

(Yes, it's true: more dog shit on my doorstep.)

Oh, You! There you are! There! at the speed of light and I love You. Please don't betray me by insisting we meet. Don't prove your infidelity by wanting too much.

Please,
jc

THE COLOR OF REVENGE

She believes everything must have a color. Therefore:

What is the color of revenge? Not red, an impulsive hue of quick anger and undeterred lust. No, revenge is slow burning, cool and calculated, blue and clean like propane. She dresses in pale blue silk, naked beneath the cool slip of a dress, nails stripped of polish, hair still wet from a good scrubbing and no cream rinse or conditioner to weight it down.

PICTURING THE PAST: PART TWO

Quiz

(1) Leave me the hell alone, will you?
But why don't you love me anymore?

(2) I just don't, that's all.
Tell me the truth.

(3) All right. I've met someone else. Satisfied?
She's younger than me—and a lot taller.

(4) How did you know that?
You're parting your hair differently.

WHEN PEOPLE SEEK EXCELLENCE THEY LOOK FOR A SIGN

Date: Fri, 05 Apr 2002 16:11:45 -0500
To: prettygrl@bohemia.cz
From: jiricech@earthlink.net
Subject: I Want You

Dear You:
Here the day begins when the sun comes up. No more lingering in bed where it is warm and smelling of sweat and cum! Yes, I masturbate. What did you expect? I'm a man with sexual energy not easily quashed. If you were here that energy would go into you--literally and figuratively. The thought of my cock in your cunt excites me even now.

But let me repeat: I don't ever want to meet you. The probability of our mutual disappointment depresses me so much I want to weep, claw at my eyes, tear at my hair, and I've wept and clawed and torn so much already.

argh!
Jirí

HOW FAST ARE YOU GOING?

(Medea appears above us in a chariot drawn by dragons.)

THE WOMAN and HER VERY BEST FRIEND are eating enormous salads at the Cheep Salad Bar[33] and talking about work and new shoes as if the war in Eastern Europe were a commercial for ***New and Improved!*** tampons. Though THE WOMAN now dislikes HER VERY BEST FRIEND to an irreversible depth, she pretends affinity. Nevertheless HER VERY BEST FRIEND senses something amiss in THE WOMAN's behavior but attributes it to PMS or gas.

Why the pretense? Because THE WOMAN has a secret that she shall soon reveal, a gleam of victory and pride in her eyes (victory in right eye, pride in left) to HER VERY BEST FRIEND who will stare in awe, she is certain, awed by her wit and intelligence, stare in awe at least up until the moment THE WOMAN says:

THE WOMAN: **Moses removed his sandals before the Burning Bush, afraid to desecrate the ground from which God arose as living flame. He knew his place in the scheme of things, humbled himself before a power so incomprehensible that its only route of manifestation was a shrub whose fire would not go out. Moses recognized omnipotence and was thusly rewarded with the power to part waters.**

---

[33] Salads again, as if eating healthy, when in fact each salad contains over 1,000 calories and 34 grams of fat, and the lettuce and other fresh vegetables have been heavily sprayed with preservatives to extend their shelf life, and the cottage and cheddar and blue cheeses were made from cows fed hormones and antibiotics in order to produce more milk. As I write this cancer cells have begun multiplying in the left breast of HER VERY BEST FRIEND while here it has just begun to rain outside my window. I can hear the trembling of leaves, whisper of grass. All birds have gone silent, and the breeze is sweet and cool and clean. Such moments make one reconsider the weight of things—not the body's weight for it will lighten to dust or ash soon enough, but the weight of what's on **THE WOMAN's** mind as she waits for HER VERY BEST FRIEND to finish yet another story about her loathsome boss. Outside it rains and there is nothing I'd rather do at this moment than stand barefoot in the wet grass, lift my face to the sky, recall the first time I stood in a summer storm, and for a tender moment believe I am once again a child weighted only by rain. Incredibly, it is this very same yearning that flashes through **THE WOMAN's** mind as she bites into a tainted snow pea, therefore missing part of **HER VERY BEST FRIEND's** I-loathe-my-boss story. Which, in hindsight, she knows was a blessing.

But I'm getting ahead of myself. A half-hour before the Moses bit—which has absolutely no relevance to this story, not even to me (who wrote it), I just like the image of Moses going barefoot, thinking the soles of his feet would somehow be cleaner than the soles of his sandals—THE WOMAN speaks:

THE WOMAN: I placed an ad in "Personals" under Men Seeking Men. I received 72 responses and replied to all of them with unbridled enthusiasm, signing Jirí's name and listing all of his phone numbers—home, office, and cell—plus his pager number and his e-mail address. I enclosed a photograph of him, the one I took at the beach last summer where he looks kind of like Rock Hudson in *Lover Come Back*.

CURIOUS MINDED Very attractive PWM, 42, over 6', 180, muscled, hung, seeks HWP SGM to explore long repressed sexual desires. Please be gentle! Respond to Ad#1022A

[34]

HER VERY BEST FRIEND is dumbfounded. She says, "I'm dumbfounded." Later that day she makes the long walk from her parking space to her office. She is preoccupied and moody. By the time she sits in her ergonomically correct chair and brushes a strand of hair from her knitted brow and picks an aphid from the Wandering Jew on her desk, she has decided that (1) THE WOMAN is insane, (2) she no longer wishes to be THE WOMAN's VERY BEST FRIEND, (3) Doris Day's acting talent was grossly underrated, and (4) she no longer wishes to be associated with THE WOMAN in any way, shape or form. Her wish will come to pass. THE WOMAN will not give a shit.

[34] PWM = Professional White Male. HWP = Height/Weight Proportionate. SGM = Single Gay Male.

AND A MOUNTAIN OF EVIDENCE TO PROVE IT

Date: Wed, 17 Apr 2002 10:50:08 -0800
To: prettygrl@bohemia.cz
From: jiricech@earthlink.net
Subject: Scatological concerns

Dear You:
Well, it's not dog shit, it's pig shit. Don't misconstrue: I'm not a shit expert. I'm not even into scatological humor. But I took quite a large pile to the local vet and had it analyzed. She, the vet, wasn't eager to accommodate my query and was for some reason upset with the *amount* I'd brought as evidence, but I paid her as much as it would have cost to surgically remove shit from a pig's anus, so she agreed to do the analysis. Pig shit! I asked her, the vet, where someone would have gotten pig shit in this city? She told me, "Well, it's not shit from a pot-bellied pig, that's for sure. The turds are too thick." (I don't think she actually used the word "turds.") "Then where?" I demanded, for I was by this time extremely vexed. The vet said, "There's a corporate pig farm up north, about two to three hours away. They have plenty of pig shit. Maybe she got the shit there." And I said, "She? She? What makes you think it's a *she* who's leaving pig shit on my doorstep?" And the vet gave a smug little snort of a laugh and said, "Who else would exact such clever revenge but A WOMAN!" Then she handed me all the pig shit in a plastic bag, which I took, though I'm not sure why.

Oh, You You You!

The whole world has gone to shit, hasn't it? For You are there (where I wish You to remain) and I love You and am lonely for the woman You are there not here where You'd be ~~ordinary~~ ~~pathetic~~ ~~redundant~~ somehow less than You are there.

love,
jirí

CHORUS: O this cannot have a happy ending!

Date: Sun, 21 Apr 2002 08:19:15 -0500
To: prettygrl@bohemia.cz
From: jiricech@earthlink.net
Subject: The Power of Myth

Dear You:
Replicating a moment from the prehistoric past, a dragon stands defiantly outside my window. If I were a coward, I'd be scared shitless. No pun intended.

jc

CHORUS: O this story will end ~~sadly~~!
" " " " " ~~madly~~!
" " " " " badly!

CRIME – BOTH ORGANIZED AND PETTY – CAN BE DIFFICULT

All right, maybe this isn't about Glauke at all. Maybe it's about Medea. But why, I ask, why not Glauke? Why do victims not pique our interest? Why only the victimizers? When we think of Susan Smith, why don't we first remember her children, wonder about them in their last moments of living, the utter disbelief in their fluttering little souls, pounding on the rear window of the car sinking into the dark dark death-water, screaming, "Mommy! Mommy! MOM-MEEEEEEE!!!" Utter disbelief as only children can disbelieve, utterly: believing the opposite more palatable story must be must be oh has to be true, doesn't it, Mommy? Mommy!?! MOM—

Worse perhaps than their deaths is the victims fading in our collective memory while their perpetrators grow to mythological proportions. And so do we love more deeply, admire more particularly, the killer in our souls?

Quiz
circle your preference:
(select only one)
prey **predator**

```
Date: Wed, 01 May 2002  19:50:38 -0600
To: prettygrl@bohemia.cz
From: jiricech@earthlink.net
Subject: Watch Out!
```

Dear You:
It must be a coincidence, some glitch in the space/time continuum, incontestable proof that we are destined for one another (as long as we keep our distance) for it can't be otherwise.

But how could you possibly think I'm the culprit? I don't even know where to get pig shit, having no idea what the hell a "corporate pig farm" is. All I can say is, if there's pig shit on your doorstep then there must be a dragon nearby. Watch your step, darling--figuratively and literally! And think of me and my own hellish sidestepping here while You are there. And tonight why don't You dream of me hovering like some future saint over You, virtually real, real enough for love, the way we love here in this clean world of emptiness.

always, always,
Jirí

THE WOMAN: Moses removed his sandals before the Burning Bush, afraid to desecrate the ground from which God arose as living flame. He knew his place in the scheme of things, humbled himself before a power so incomprehensible that its only route of manifestation was a shrub whose fire would not go out. Moses recognized omnipotence and was thusly rewarded with the power to part waters.

Maybe Moses does have something to do with this story after all. Moses kneeling before the burning bush, a bush aflame, flame as the voice of God: vengeful God who could and believe me would kick some major ass when it came to exacting revenge. Frogs and locusts and disease and fiery (again fire!) hailstorms?

We don't need a psychopath to teach vengeance. We have God.

HOW FAST ARE YOU GOING?

(Medea appears above us in a chariot drawn by dragons.)

THINGS CERTAINLY AREN'T WHAT THEY USED TO BE

No. Certainly not.

When a jet-lagged body thinks it's morning not even a hearty dinner will help. Not even the chiming of church bells in the piazza nor a slap in the face nor ice water on the genitals. Will help.

Yes, after a long night of killing on the other side of the world, THE WOMAN is tired but can neither sleep nor stay awake. She hovers somewhere in between, caught in a bardo state wherein reality and dreams overlap so precisely that there is no distinguishing fact from fiction/fiction from fact. Much as in the case of a reader who suspects that the author's inventions/intentions are more deeply seated in truth than imagination.

Thus THE WOMAN wonders if, in a small third-floor apartment in Prague, crumpled in a corner like a rag doll carelessly tossed aside, a pretty young Bohemian woman by the name of You is really burning to death inside a *tunica molesta* or if in fact it was all just a fantasy to mollify the desperation rising inside her like a wet wasp from a cracked mud-heart.

CHORUS: No Woman could resist that gown.

Not even You who thinks herself above crass materialism. And so You put on the lovely dress, the surprise gift, and stand before the long oval mirror admiring Your beauty. And You think it must be love—an astonishing and welcome form of self-love—that makes Your skin burn beneath the gown. Until the burning/ the loving intensifies, grows unbearable beneath the fine fabric that smells faintly of petroleum. And it is then the world converges—scraps of stories loosed in time folding into one another, gaping seams stitched tight and catching fire. Fire of Your love, God's voice afire, You are on fire and not even a cold shower will put it out.

No. No.

> "[P]etroleum, sulphur, and lime…ignite and burn in ways similar to the descriptions of Medea's…cloak. Petroleum products are notorious for flowing, clinging, unquenchable flames…. Sprinkled with water, quicklime becomes slaked lime, which can generate enough heat to cause spontaneous combustion, and water would feed these flames."
>
> —*Archaeology Magazine,* March/April 1997

CHORUS: Ah, revenge! Sweet revenge! Sticky revenge! Humanity's favorite pastime. Exxon never had it so good.

Jesus-God-and-Mary-too THE WOMAN is tired! She collapses onto the bed and thinks of Doris Day in *Lover Come Back,* there at the movie's end where Doris is pregnant on a gurney, being wheeled into the hospital delivery room just as Rock arrives to rescue her from solitude and single motherhood and silly hats. *Rescue her not necessarily because he loves her,* thinks THE WOMAN, *but because he knocked her up.* She lays her hands on her flat belly and thinks, *If only I'd gotten pregnant. Oh, well. Too late now. Too late.*

She stares at a water stain on the ceiling of this foreign hotel room—in Vienna? Budapest? Sofia?—and thinks how its shape reminds her of him, the man for whom she feels such passion that to call it "love" seems a denigration, a bastardization of the soul. Water stain resembling his face with chin scar and lazy eyelid and one crooked tooth on the bottom like a weary young soldier no longer able to stand at attention.

"Ten-hut!" she hears: rasping of knife on whetstone.

"Ten-hut!" fading now.

Fading: "Ten-hut!"

"Ten-hut!"

"Ten-hut!"

special advertising section

If you think you have to take responsibility for your actions, think again.

Owning up to your own shit? That's just not the way we do things here.

No matter how much you lie, cheat and steal, you can always blame it on someone else. Your employee, your boss, your VERY BEST FRIEND. Even your dog.

That's right. Your dog.

The same dog that ate your homework in third grade is all grown up. Now it can shred documents, erase state's evidence, perjure, embezzle, bribe, extort, scam, blackmail, swindle, defraud, fuck over & up & off. Even murder.

Talented dog. Lucky you.

Woof, woof.

HELLIBURTON

making money hand over fist

Jirí Cêch's Cuba Deposition

Longtime Cuban Leader Fidel Castro yodeled, "Yoo-hoo! Jirí! I see you!" while accusing American real estate developer Jirí Cêch, formerly of the former Czechoslovakia, now The Czech Republic, of spying for the United States. The U.S. subsequently accused Cêch of spying for Cuba.

Why the fuck would anybody look at me and think, "He's a spy!" I write poetry while sitting shitting on the john, for chrissake. I read *People* magazine for the pictures not the stories. I build suburban houses that make the landscape look like the great god of kitsch took a shit while camping in the woods. Oh yes, I give them what they want, my hamster-head clients with bad taste who leave a bad taste in my mouth every time I leave them standing inside the imaginary walls of their house thinking how a fucking Jenair stove and triple-pane Andersen windows are going to improve their marriage: make him come harder; her come period. Fucking idiots! They sense my disdain but think because I speak with a Czech accent they might be wrong. They're not. I disdain. Oh yes, fucking A, I do disdain. But it has nothing to do with government, nothing to do with patriotism—or lack thereof. Hey, man, I love this country. I'm rich. I drink a bottle of Château Lafite-Rothschild every night, have my teeth cleaned every six months, get a massage once a week, facial every three weeks, manicure once a month—twice if I've had to lift a finger, which is seldom. I'm a desk jockey, chair hugger, office booger. I'm so comfortable I'd have a fat ass if I didn't have a personal fitness trainer to keep me trim and toned. But a spy? Shit. You want to know why I went to Cuba, I'll tell you: to fuck their women.

Oops. Sorry.

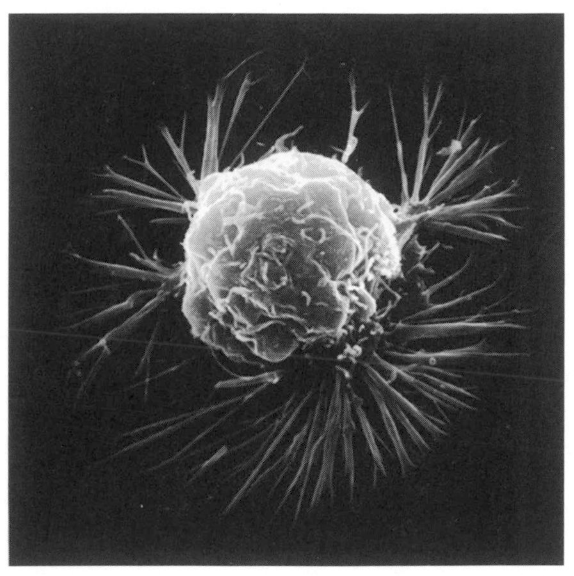

35

SPRING HAS SPRUNG

Jesus, what it must be like to die in the spring!

is what she thought. Just then her dying neighbor across the street looked up from the flower bed she was tending and smiled. Odd smile. Happy. No. More than happy. Calm. No. More than calm. Content? Yes, utterly. Utterly content. Smile.

I've never felt content in my life.

is what she thought. And

Will you feel so content after you're dead?

is what she wanted to ask her neighbor. And rather suddenly, no, quite suddenly, as if a piano had just fallen out of a *757* en route to Prague and landed on her head...*that* suddenly, she loathed her

[35] Magnification illustrating "breast cancer cells with intercellular boundaries on bead surface and aggregates of cells achieving 3-dimensional growth outward from bead." Credit: Dr. Jeanne Becker, University of South Florida. (Source: Science @ NASA (http://science.nasa.gov/newhome)

dying neighbor. So that when she returned her dying neighbor's smile it was tight and oily. Disingenuous.

Cut your face in half, there's a phony smile on the bottom and genuine hate-filled eyes on the top.

You should be ashamed of yourself.

Should be
Should be
Should
Sh

You can never have too many beginnings!

Your neighbor across the street looks up from the flower bed she's tending, tending with great care, the tulips just now sprouting from the black dirt, the sedum returning green after a long brown winter playing dead. With great care, sweeping the dry oak leaves from around the new green shoots, picking out the litter of newspaper and Styrofoam and bits of cellophane blown in from god-knows-where. Carefully replenishing the mulch: cedar: scent: She raises a handful to her nose, inhales, closes her eyes, smiles. Looks up from the flowerbed, over her left shoulder to see you standing on your front porch staring at her in a yellow hat you know covers a bald head, at you thinking how the yellow hat looks so cheerful against the periwinkle blue of her house she painted last fall, right after she learned the cancer had come back *en force,* was in her lymph nodes now, her liver, nothing they could do though they fed her chemicals anyway as if she were a Wandering Jew who just needed Miracle-Gro to get better.

She, your neighbor, has made it this far, into spring. Though she knows she will be dead when the chrysanthemums explode to yellow blooms, she plants them anyway. By seed. As if it's important she be there in their beginning: heat and oil and sweat of flesh the first world of seven worlds flowers must past through to reach heaven: a place of light drifting across the plains of infinity.

You watch her brush her hands satisfied with efficacy, smiling wistfully at a future where chrysanthemums bloom in her absence, drop seeds, bloom again.

Boss: What's this word here?
You: Efficacy.
Boss: What the hell does that mean?
You: It means having the power to produce an effect. You wrote "I have my doubts about his efficiency with the client." Within the letter's context I think you meant efficacy.
Boss: Don't tell me what I meant. You're not paid to tell me what I mean, you're paid to do what I say, you're paid to type what I write, not to criticize my vocabulary. Is that understood?
You: I wasn't criticizing, I was just—
Boss: If I wrote efficiency then I damn well meant efficiency. Understood?
You: So do you want me to retype it?
Boss: No sense wasting time. Send it out the way it is.

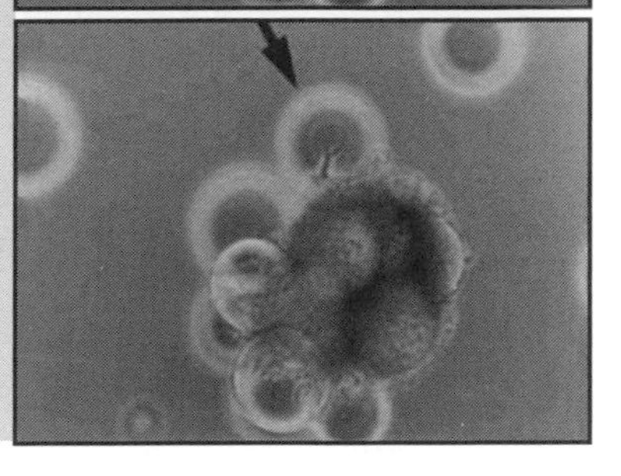

OF ALL THE THINGS THAT CAN KEEP YOU UP NIGHTS . . .

esprit d'escalier is the most persistent. Earlier in the day her BOSS whom she loathes scoops her heart out with a dull spoon. Now she tosses and turns in bed, attempting to alter the past:

Boss: If I wrote efficiency, then I damn well meant efficiency. Is that understood?
You: I was only trying to help.

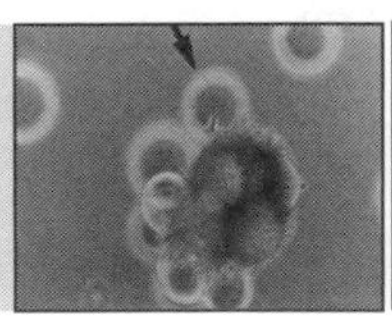

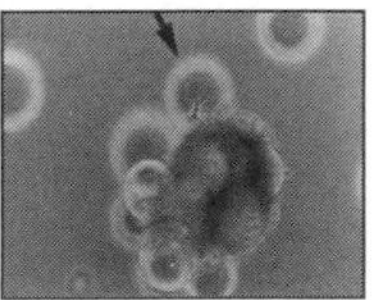

[36]

36 "Tumor cells aggregate on microcarrier beads (indicated by arrow)." Credit: Dr. Jeanne Becker, University of South Florida. Source: Science @ NASA (http://science.nasa.gov/newhome)

Boss:	If I wrote efficiency, then I damn well meant efficiency. Is that understood?
You:	I was only trying to make you look good.

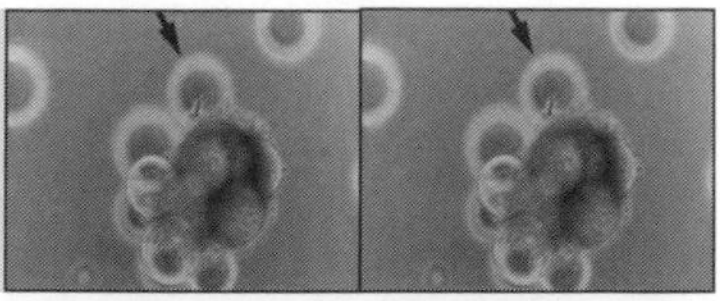

Boss:	If I wrote efficiency, then I damn well meant efficiency. Is that understood?
You:	I was only trying to make a silk purse out of a sow's ear.

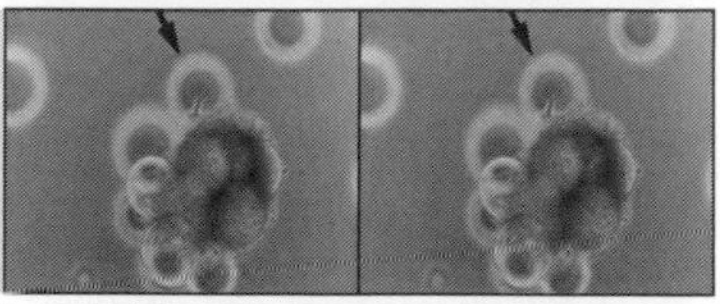

Boss:	If I wrote efficiency —
You:	Wrote?!? Gimme a break, you can barely spell your name.

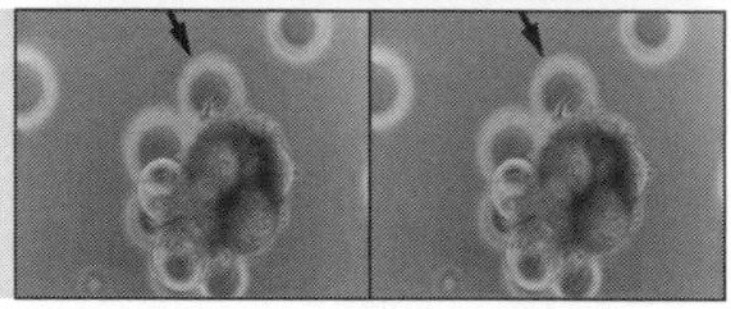

Boss:	If I wrote efficiency, then I damn well meant efficiency. Is that understood?
You:	Shut the fuck up, I quit.

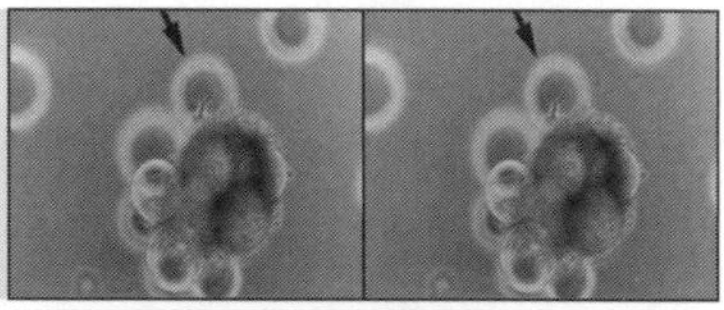

Boss:	If I wrote efficiency, then I damn well meant efficiency. Is that understood?
You:	Why don't you go fuck yourself, you goddamn overpromoted addlepated ignoramus. Oh, and would you like a DICTIONARY to interpret that sentence, you fucking loser suckass butt-wipe cocksucker!

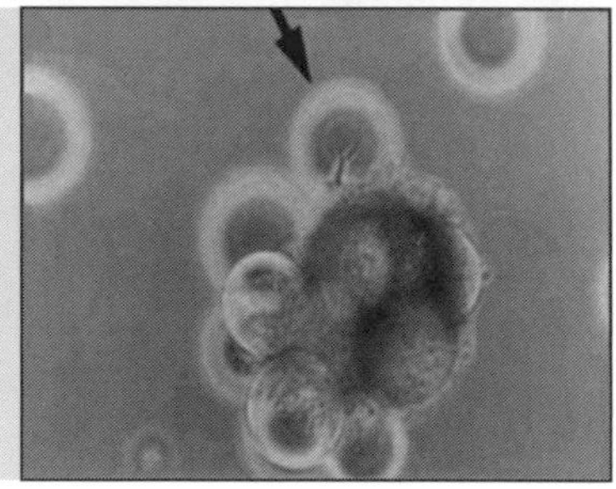

Finally her thoughts turn to homicide, or rather **ACTS OF GOD** perpetrated by She, Goddess of Justice, Queen of the Damned and Trodden and Nine-to-Fivers or -Eighters,[37] Omnipotent Potentatette, and she imagines HER BOSS WHOM SHE LOATHES strolling down the long hallway of the 21st floor when an earthquake with a magnitude of 9.9 on the Richter Scale rips the building apart, the

[37] President __ of the telecommunications company __ sends a memo to all employees stating, among other dull but noxious edicts, that "although the work week is officiously [sic?] 40 hours per week, I expect all of us [read: 'you underfuckerlings'] to put in not less than 55 hours per week in order to boost productivity and consequencially [sic] declining stock prices in an incertain [sic] market."

floor opening up under BOSS's feet and BOSS plummeting into the magma-roiling pit of **HELL ON EARTH** where BOSS shall live out BOSS's eternity, missing the Second Coming entirely and regretting every shitty-BOSS-scourge BOSS cursed on employees, amen Amen *Amen* AMEN!

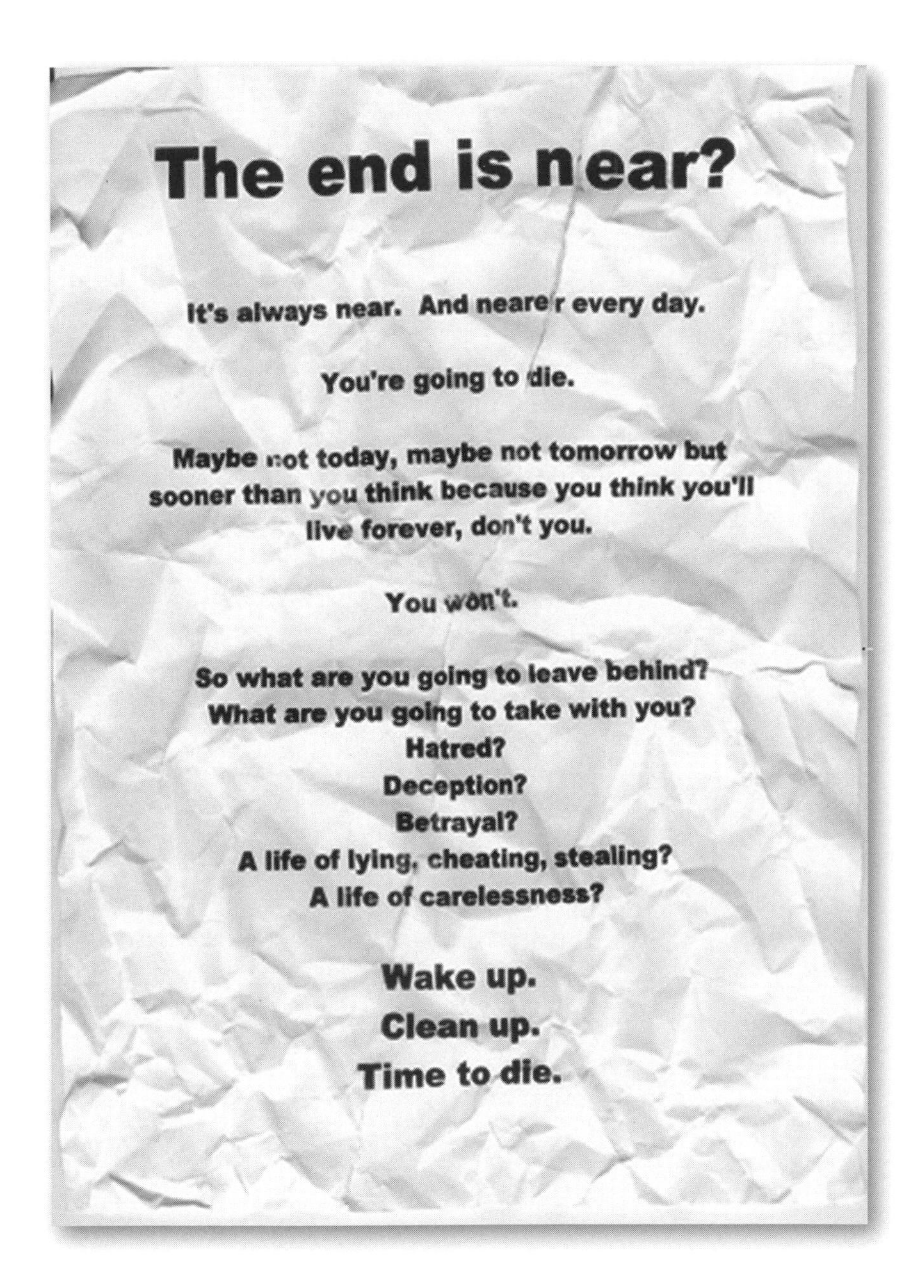

THE DEVIL SMOKES CIGARS IN THE 700 CLUB

The leaflet guy is back. Or maybe it's a gal. Gal Friday. Out to save 700 souls on her 45-minute lunch break. 700 leaflets appearing like magic under 700 windshield wipers on 700 cars in the parking garage.

She can hear the chainsaws growling, tree trunks spitting sawdust, raw wood cracking, clatter of leaves twigs branches bark upon the underbrush vines ferns wildflowers moss. Somewhere on the once-a-forest floor a scarab beetle feels the rush of wind presaging death manifest in a falling pine and tries to flee its fate but the pine is big and the beetle's legs are small and there is only shadow shadow deeper than before the lumberjacks came before there is nothing.

Family SCARABAEIDAE, genera Dynastines. Best known for their immense size and the amazing horn-like structures that the males of many species possess. These structures are used mainly for defending feeding sites and during strength contests with other males over mates during the breeding season. Though the vast majority of these "rhinoceros beetles" are to be found deep within the great equatorial rain forests of the planet, there are a few species that live in more temperate latitudes such as NORTH AMERICA and Europe.... The larvae of dynastines primarily feed on the soft, decaying wood of dead trees. The larvae increase in size greatly as they progress. They often require many months to complete their growth, undergo METAMORPHOSIS within a protective cell, and then RE-ENTER THE WORLD as adult beetles.

— Source: www.naturalworlds.org

DOCTOR says, "I've got bad news."

Sh
Sh
Shadow shadow deeper falling.

"This is the route," he says, pointing to the line zigzagging across the CT-Scan.

IN WHICH YOU REACT TO THE LONG ROAD OF UNCERTAINTY AHEAD BY SCREAMING

I understand how you hate the world. Want to trip it as it saunters by smug knowing it's forever while you're just a flicker—sun caught in a speeding car's chrome. There. Then not there. The chrome not even warmed by your light.

Scream scream.

There's a place in your head like a windowless room where you scream to fill in the hole left by silence. Bury the fear in your screaming. Sure, let them shake their heads, those with their flesh not yet rotting; they'll know/rot soon enough. Know the ecstasy of a voice unleashed like the god of Moses.

> *O Eternal, what god is there like you, who is like you, so gloriously supreme, so awful, whom we praise for extraordinary deeds?*

Eternal? You cannot believe in life beyond your death though you desire. And when you are dead, when your blood has been drained and your eyes sewn shut, and the nails of your hands blush black you will be only dead.

Absent from the world.
is what she thinks and picks an aphid from the leaf of the Wandering Jew and crushes it between her fingers.

A fate worse than hell.
is what she thinks.

At least in pain there's living.

"I don't believe in hell," she tells her BOSS, apropos of nothing. "Except the one here now," and she points the index finger of her right hand and maneuvers it around the office like a divining rod seeking water—and there is water everywhere: BOSS, Computer, Time Sheet (so much damn time wasted, wasted time recorded in the Book... no, the *Database* of Judgment), water even in the Wandering Jew with its aphids devouring—until her finger turns backward, curls backward, points backward at her breasts with their lumps, and she says,

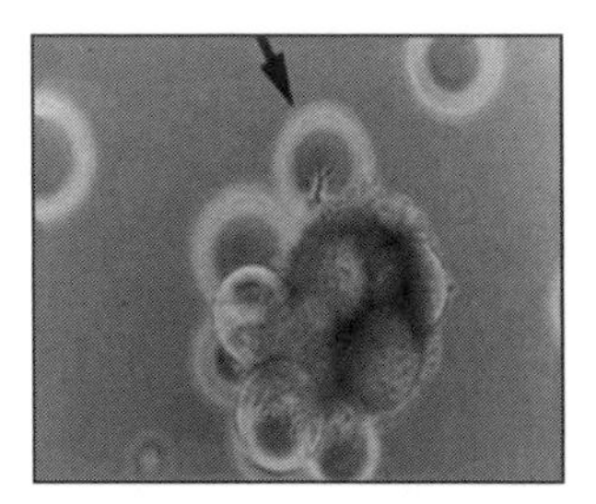

"Hell, metastasizing."

She cannot possibly remember them all, all the lumps blooming from coffee and push-up bras and homogenized hormone-laded milk and a gene whose sole purpose is to shiver awake when kissed by environmental toxins and rise and kiss awake another gene whose sole purpose is to grow lumps in breasts.

I cannot possibly remember them all but I remember my first—yes, remember like a first lover who takes me against my will yet I harbor a secret desire for him nevertheless. My first at fourteen: big tender globe of fluid grown hard, tucked inside my armpit. I told no one because to acknowledge it was to make it real.

I told no one and it went away. Others replaced it, coming with their courting gifts of terror, going with their parting gifts of relief. And somewhere in between: God and all the scheming negotiating conniving bargaining that led me to believe prayer would save me, as long as the prayers were long enough, heartfelt enough, original enough, pretty enough, frequent enough, good enough for God.

I told no one. I prayed good.

This lump was different: pearl under the skin. Oysters of flesh on the sand of the bones. Bauble bead gem sunk in mud. Dig it out dig it out mining for gold those researchers with their white lab coats their stainless steel voices their eyes that never meet your eyes—*O do not see the human, the humanity, or you'll never make the cut*—and

Look at me goddamn it!

is what she thought. And

If I fire my doctor will the next one kill me out of vengeance?

is what she thought. And again

Pearl.

She once had a horse named Pearl. Shetland pony. Silvery-white and fat-bellied and interested only in eating, consuming—oats, carrots, corn, apples, clover, grass. One day Pearl consumed too much fescue and foundered: hooves growing long so fast, blooming up and curling back like lilies into the silvery-white legs, the white bones, until she could not walk and the father hauled Pearl away and sold her for $20 to a slaughterhouse where she was shot and skinned and ground into dog food.

She is surprised by how much love she can still summon for a horse dead so many years but distinct in her mind in the shimmering green pastures lit with dew in the summer morning in the past that is unreachable, untouchable ghost, the ghost of Pearl.

The one time she tried to run away from home was on Pearl's back. Less than a mile down the dirt road Pearl spied sweet clover alongside the ditch and would not walk farther. She dismounted and sat on the bank above the ditch and watched Pearl eat, waiting for Father and Mother to come looking for her. They never came. Eventually Pearl got full or thirsty or bored, and girl and pony headed home.

She can still smell horse sweat. Hear the long silvery-white tail swishing at flies. The comforting *crunch-crunch-crunch* of masticating teeth. See her reflection in a brown-black eye that seemed to always look beyond this world into another: long steady glimpse of perpetuity.

> *You lay your hand upon the hospital gown and pretend it's Pearl's winter coat beneath your fingers. You cry soundlessly thinking of the light in your pony's eyes doused. You would like Pearl back to run away for good. This time, not turn for home.*

WHEN YOU KNOW IT'S REAL

Fear is the worst of it. Makes you dizzy. Weak in the knees. Hair on the back of your neck bristles. Sometimes fear's so big it fills your whole life tight and you can't breathe and you think the cancer's in your lungs now fat lumps of consuming cells and you're suffocating so you call your MD who X-rays your chest and it at least is fine so your MD prescribes Xanax and you take one and then two and then three and go to sleep for twelve hours of dreamlessness and when you wake up you think it's dawn but it's dusk, so now there's just you and soon the looming dark and silence and somewhere behind a wall in the room of your mind fear still pounds its meaty fists against your heart that now beats fast and irregular and you think the cancer is in your heart now you're having a heart attack so you call 911 and the EMTs arrive and after a while your heart slows to 66 bpm but they take you to ER anyway because you have cancer and the ER RNs hook you up to an EKG and take your BP and everything seems fine and you notice how safe you feel in the ER with the RNs and LPNs in their sea green scrubs and you realize that except for the cancer there's nothing wrong with you but fear and you ask to go home and they release you and the night is very crisp like you never felt before and you don't take a cab you walk home which is 12 miles and by the time you arrive at 5:37 AM the sun's coming up and you're covered with dew.

AND THEN THE OTHER DEMONS ARRIVE

ART THERAPIST says, "Why don't you try using some color?"

It's my goddamn drawing.

is what you think.

It's my goddamn cancer.

is what you mumble. And you want to hit ART THERAPIST with your fists, hit everything, hit yourself until you bleed and the blood says you're still alive.

ART THERAPIST nods and says, "Much better!"

DOCTOR SAYS

"...new treatment that appears to have some positive results in some...combination of radiation and chemotherapy for six months ...basically destroys your immune system with the cancer but... fatigue, nausea, skin discoloration, dryness, hair loss...best I can offer at this stage, so..."

CHEMOTHERAPY & RADIATION ALTERNATIVES

1. Breast Cancer Therapy Group
2. Art Therapy
3. Yoga
4. Transcendental Meditation
5. Focused Breathing Exercises
6. Stress Reduction Class
7. Tai Chi
8. Macrobiotic Diet
9. Green Tea
10. Chinese Herbs
11. Echinacea
12. Vitamin Therapy
13. Visualization
14. Acupuncture
15. Cranial-Sacrum Massage
16. Past-Life Regression
17. Smudging
18. Pray without Ceasing
19. Ozone Therapy
20. Colonic Cleansing
21. Crystals
22. Magnets

Suddenly it seems that everyone from your past is in your present and on TV. What they mean by your life passing before your eyes? Like the Czech BOYFRIEND-YOU-NEVER-LIKED of a FRIEND-YOU-NO-LONGER-LIKE who was arrested in Cuba for spying, the Czech, that is, Jirí Cêch. Which makes you laugh. And you feel momentarily healed.

23. Watch Comedies

And then, coincidentally (but you no longer believe in coincidence, your mind regressed to a primitive intuitive-laden state when women understood the net of the universe without having to take a course in physics) the FRIEND-YOU-NO-LONGER-LIKE is on the same TV news program, arrested for attempted murder somewhere in Prague and you stare at her as she's escorted by police, and you notice that her hair looks dull and unkempt, and she's wearing green which does not compliment her skin tone and it all makes you depressed and nostalgic for things you cannot name.

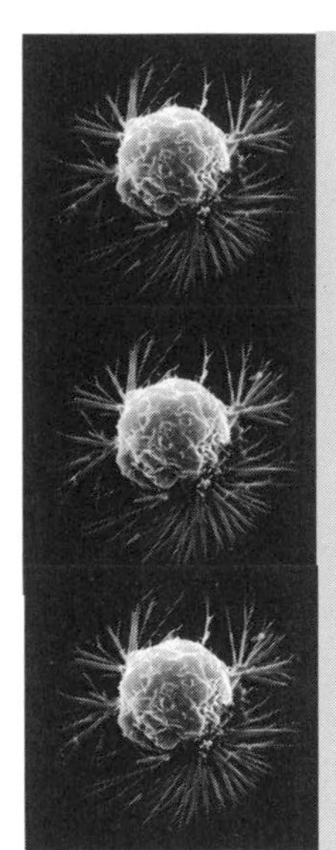

Boss: I need you to be at the top of your game in your head even if you're not tops in your body. Understand?
You: ...
Boss: Anyway. There are some typos in this proposal. I need you to fix them.
You: "Irregardless" is not a word.
Boss: Are we going to have this argument again?
You: And "profits are impacted by loose shipping timeframes" sounds like profits are constipated, as in impacted bowels. Whatever "loose timeframes" means.
Boss: ...
You: It's "profits are affected by." Plain, simple, accurate English.
Boss: You need this job, don't you?
You: ...
Boss: Well. Then. End of argument.

25. Kill My Boss!

God is not a vending machine.

You expect to put in a prayer and an answer will pop out.

Specifically, the answer you want.

Specifically, *what* you want *when* you want it.

God is not a fast-food joint, either.

Pray every day for other people in need. and you'll be okay.

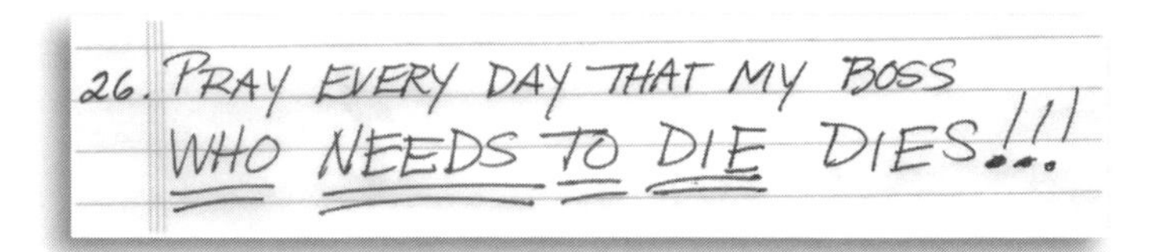

You say:	Are you the one who's been leaving this shit on everybody's windshield?
He says:	Not me. It's probably so-and-so down in accounting. She's a Catholic.

You say:	Are you the one who's been leaving this shit on everybody's windshield?
She says:	No, but I think whoever's doing it is probably evangelical.

You say:	Are you the one who's been leaving this shit on everybody's windshield?
She says:	What if I am?
You say:	Are you?
She says:	Maybe, maybe not.
You say:	Yes or no?
She says:	No, but what if I was?
You say:	I'd cram it down your fucking throat.
She says:	You're crazy.
You say:	I'm dying.

You put the leaflet in your 700 Club file folder with the other leaflets and close the drawer and fold your hands on your desk and stare at the Wandering Jew, searching for aphids, but there are none.

I don't want to die here.

is what you think. And

I don't want to die.

is what you think. And

I won't!

THE GOSPEL ACCORDING TO YOU

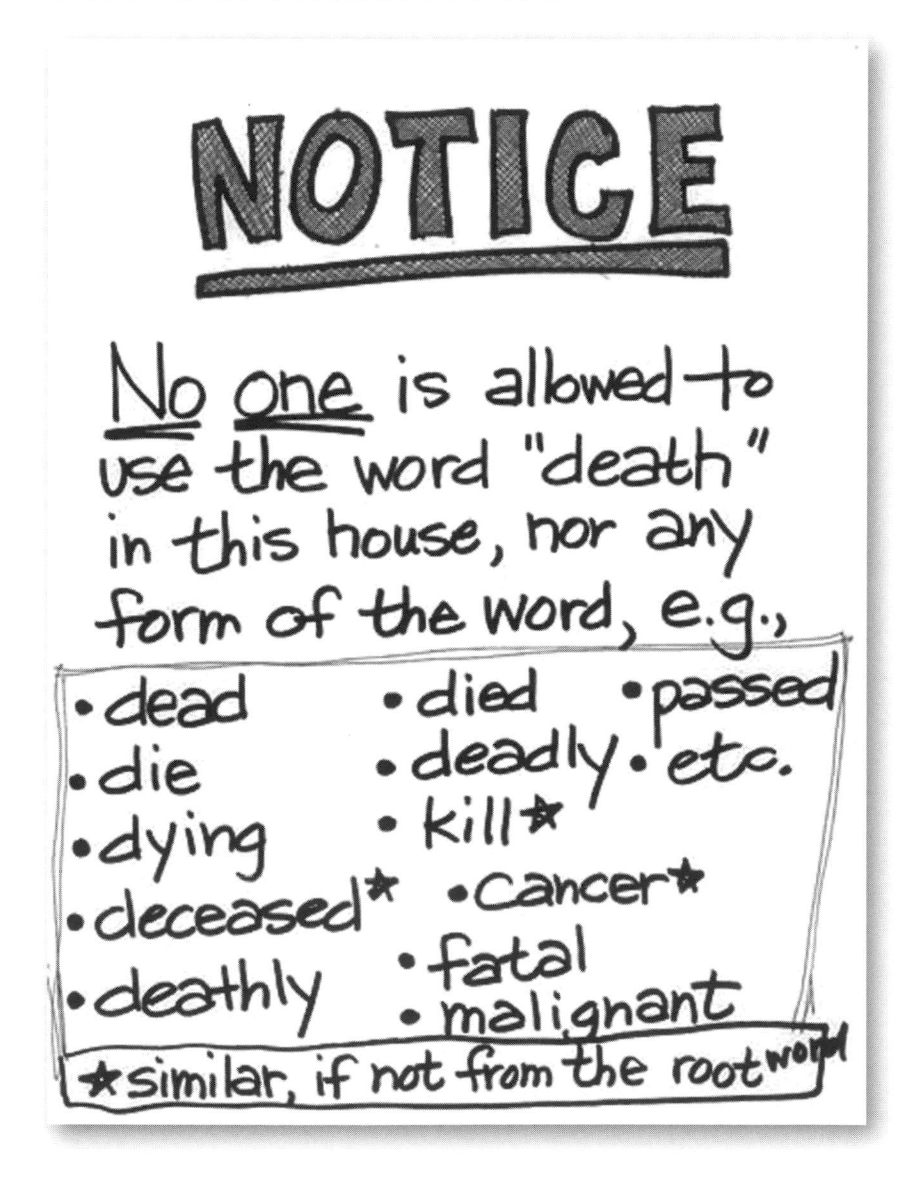

NEW SORTA BEST FRIEND says, "Hey, oh my god, you can't believe what I got!"

Cancer?

is what you think. But say

What?

"Two tickets to the *John Edward Crossing Over* show. Wanna go? "

27. Go to "John Edward Crossing Over"
(www.johnedward.net)

TRANSCRIPT

"JOHN EDWARD CROSSING OVER"

TAPING DATE: OCTOBER 15

JOHN EDWARD: Okay, I'm in this area over here. Right here. [Points to center section.]

I've got a younger female, not a mother, not an aunt. A sister, like a sister, who's crossed over. She's on the same level as… [Indicates a horizontal line with his right hand.]

She's like a sister but I don't get that she's related. Like a friend maybe or…like a friend. Her name is Pam or Pamela or… I'm getting a P-M sound like… Pamela? Pam? … Does this sound familiar to any of you. [Looks at audience.]

I'm in this section right here. [Points to center section.]

There. Right there. [Indicates two women in top row of center section.]

Did you two come together?

[Women nod yes.]

JOHN: But you're not related.

FIRST WOMAN: No. We work together.

JOHN: So one of you knows a Pam or Pamela who's passed?

[Women look at each other and shake their heads no.]

JOHN: I'm pretty sure I'm with one of you. [Pause as he concentrates.] Okay, there's a yellow hat. A *very* yellow hat, bright yellow, like a… And she's…she had cancer in this area [indicates chest]. I don't know if it's breast cancer? But… [pause as he concentrates] I see a dark area in the chest and then in this area [indicates his waist] like the kidneys or liver or… [urgently] It's a very yellow hat, it's important, and there's no…there's no hair under it. She's bald. [frustrated] One of you knows this.

JOHN: Yellow flowers, too. Like those…what are those big fat yellow flowers called? Mums. I'm getting big yellow mums the same color as the yellow hat.

SECOND WOMAN: I didn't know her name.

JOHN: What?

SECOND WOMAN: She was my neighbor and she died of cancer, but I never knew her name, I'm ashamed to say it.

JOHN: So you understand the yellow hat?

SECOND WOMAN: Yes. She wore it at the end, after she'd lost all her hair.

JOHN: [relieved] Okay, whew! So I knew I was in the right area. And she's… Her name is Pamela, by the way. [laughter] Or Pam. She wants you to know that, and she's telling me it's okay that you…that you… [puzzled] Did you have bad… I don't know how else to say this… [pause] Okay, I'm just going to say it. You didn't know her, right?

SECOND WOMAN: No, we were neighbors but, no. We never spoke.

JOHN: But you were angry with her because she… because she had cancer?

SECOND WOMAN: [Nods. Starts to cry.] It wasn't… Not exactly the cancer, but… She seemed so happy at the end, I just…and I was… She painted her house bright blue, like a bluebird, and wore the yellow hat, and planted flowers in her garden right up until the day they hauled her…the ambulance came for the last time, and she was dying and so happy, so *content* and I was living and miserable.

JOHN: [gently] Okay. Well, there's a reason, then, why she's coming through to you today. She telling me… [puzzled] This is personal. This is a personal question, but do you have breast cancer, too?

SECOND WOMAN: [nods yes]

JOHN: Well, she's telling you to… I get this image of… You know those people who dive off those high, and I mean *really* high cliffs? Into the water? That's what I'm seeing, but not like a scary thing, like a—an adventure, a thrill. It's like she saying you need to just let go, you know, you need—

SECOND WOMAN: I understand.

JOHN: —to stop being afraid and find your own yellow hat.

SECOND WOMAN: [nods]

JOHN: Okay, she's pulling back. Just know that she saw this as her opportunity to come through and help you through your own difficult illness. Okay?

SECOND WOMAN: Okay. Thank you.

JOHN: Thank you.

The Egyptians believed in an afterlife. But it was a life without sunlight, a life of perpetual night.

Every night now the possum waddles out of the chrysanthemums growing wild across the street alongside the bright blue house for sale and empty except for furniture stained rank with the smell of a dying woman's last breaths and shits and pisses. The possum crosses the street, enters your yard, pauses a moment to stare at you sitting in the porch swing, trying to detect the predator's stink, the stink of the living, the gorgeous stink of life, and smelling nothing waddles forward, past your flower bed where only white stones grow, and slugs upon the stones, trailing their wet silver. And then moves on, the possum, ruler of night and six-legged insects.

But this time you rise from the swing just as the possum nears the bed of stones and you snap your fingers and clap your hands once and say, "Hey, fucker."

And the possum stiffens and falls over onto its side, still as a two-day corpse.

You go and squat over it, daring it to move. It doesn't. Barely breathes. Eyes open, staring, unblinking. You poke it with a finger, tentative at first, then hard. The muscles beneath the soft fur are rigid with pretend death. You snap your finger in front of the possum's eyes. It doesn't blink.

"Way to go," you say, and smile.

The next night and every night after that until the weather cools, you lie on your side in your yard, barely breathing, eyes open, unblinking, staring at nothing that will be here soon enough. Let the fear swell inside you like the gas bloat of afterdeath until it no longer hurts, until it is comfortable: All you know. All you want to be.

The possum waddles by as if you were a blade of grass.

After you're dead they will refer to you as "The late...."

Late. As if for a party.

> There will come a time when you are too weak to stand to walk to the bathroom and the bowels let go and the bladder empties and the bed is wet and you're lying in your own shit and a friend comes and says *It's all right it's okay* and bathes you and changes the sheets and strokes your bald head and kisses you good-night even though it's day and not good at all.

By now the house across the street is inhabited by someone else, a couple of young professionals who paint the clapboard a terrible brown.

They dug up the yellow chrysanthemums. Replaced them with rocks.

YOU ARE LATE FOR A PARTY

Someone has slipped another flier under your windshield wiper. You say, "Jesus!" Fold the flier into quarters and shove it into your purse. At the party you drink and dance. You grind your pelvis. You swing your hips. You shake and shimmy and imagine your breasts real: young buds not yet bloomed, cancer-free. You close your eyes and remember dancing alone in your bedroom when you were seven years old pretending to be a go-go girl a hullabaloo girl in your hullabaloo boots groovy chick in your love beads fringe vest fishnet stockings ID bracelet bandanna ankh.

You arrive. Late. Jirí Cêch is there. Just released from custody. Waving an autograph from Fidel Castro.

Jirí says, "You look hot, tonight, woman," and flips that big Czech hand of his as if

The black **~~W~~hole** in the **~~Wide~~ World**

were nothing more than gnats swarming/breeding.

You say that to all the girls, Jirí.

is what you say. And think

Oh, what the hell.

And Jirí grins. Winks. Slicks back his hair.

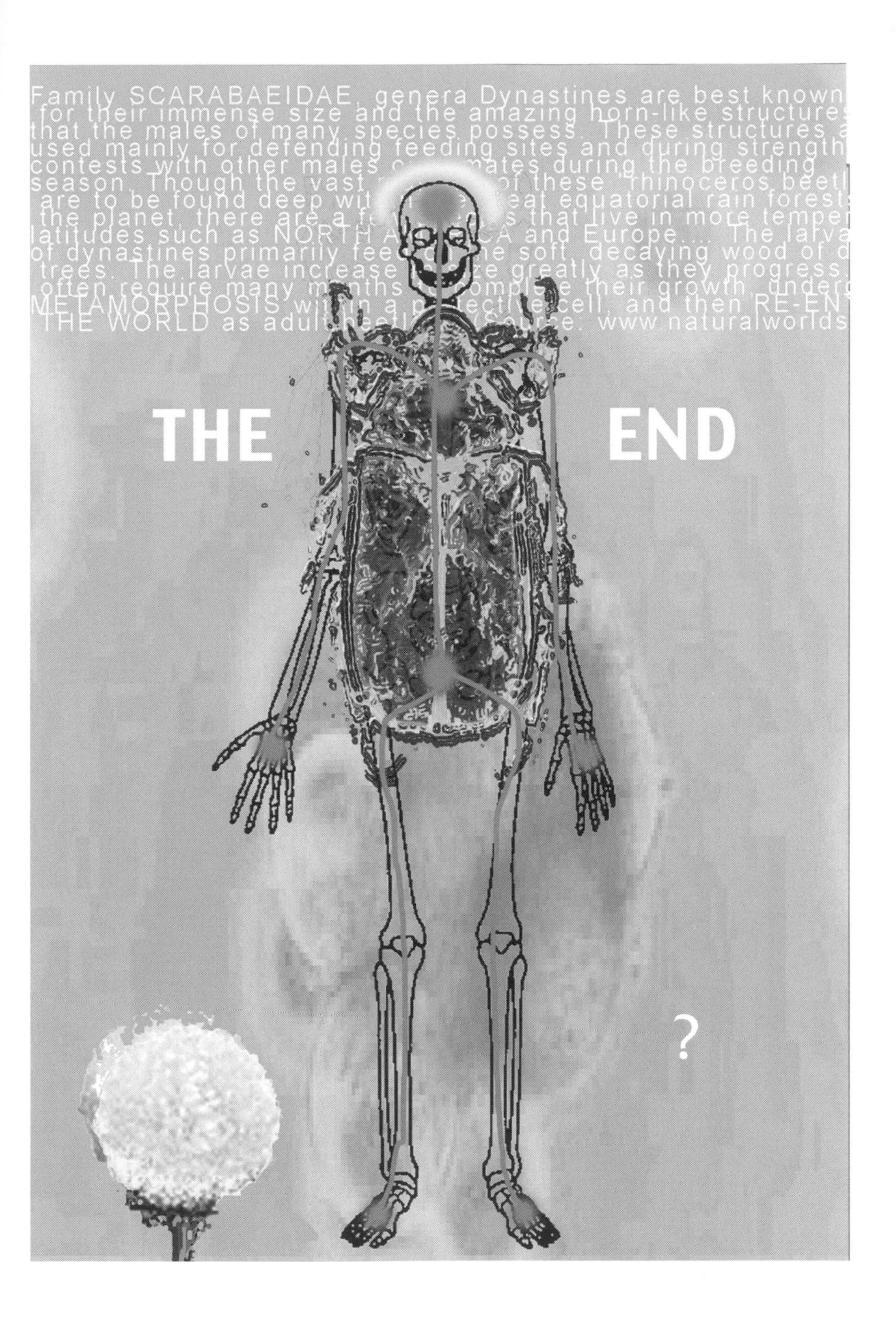
Family SCARABAEIDAE, genera Dynastines are best known
for their immense size and the amazing horn-like structure
that the males of many species possess. These structures
used mainly for defending feeding sites and during strength
contests with other males
mates during the breeding
season. Though the vast
of these "rhinoceros beetl
are to be found deep wit
eat equatorial rain forest
the planet, there are a fe
s that live in more temper
latitudes such as NORTH A
CA and Europe.... The larva
of dynastines primarily fee
he soft, decaying wood of d
trees. The larvae increase
ze greatly as they progress.
often require many m
their growth, under
METAMORPHOSIS wit
cell, and then RE-EN
THE WORLD as adult
(Source: www.naturalworlds
THE
END
?

Oh no.

You Forgot.
Today is your kid's birthday and you have a terminal illness.
It's not too late to gift wrap the life insurance policy.

Scarlet Ibis Life Insurance
Because even cremation is expensive™

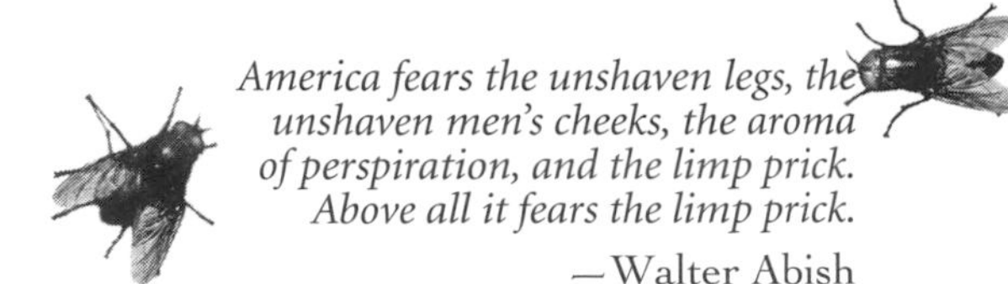

America fears the unshaven legs, the unshaven men's cheeks, the aroma of perspiration, and the limp prick. Above all it fears the limp prick.

—Walter Abish

In Case You Haven't Noticed I'm Not Wearing Any Clothes

Now You Can Forget Forever The Pain, Effort & Expense of Having a Large, Manly Penis!

THE DEFENDANT does not find it strange that he has never been to the zoo, that he has never seen a chimpanzee in the flesh-n-fur, never watched through triple-strength plate glass windows as a chimp pokes its hemorrhoidal asshole then repeatedly smells its fingertips. He does not consciously think about chimpanzees.

Not any more.

But once upon a funny time he had a big stuffed toy chimp he named Mister Butcher that had a plastic face and hands and an open mouth into which fit, perfectly, a plastic half-peeled banana that was fused to Mister Butcher's plastic left hand. Mister Butcher wore white plastic sneakers with white laces, and plaid flannel shorts with red suspenders. The shorts were sewn to Mister Butcher's crotch. The boy then, who is now a man, more or less, more less than more, defending himself against charges he does not fully comprehend, *Why don't they use plain simple English!? Cause they're all trying to screw me, that's why, goddamn Jew lawyer shysters!...*

yes, *that* boy discovered seams when he tried to peek down Mister Butcher's waistband and up the legs of Mister Butcher's shorts. The toy chimp did not have a penis, deduced the boy, already mechanical-minded, somewhere in the jackhammer future his name stitched on a blue-collar job. Or maybe, he thought, Mister Butcher had a penis so small it couldn't be felt through the plaid flannel shorts. The boy himself had a small penis—tiny tendril of pink flesh and blood—but not so tiny he couldn't feel it through his thick denim trousers. In fact, he liked to feel it through his thick denim trousers, and through his Fruit-of the-Loom cotton briefs, and through his mother's pink satiny nightgowns. And as he felt his tiny tendril he quietly hooted and grunted like a chimp, imagining he was Mister Butcher, but real, with an enormous penis and barefoot and hairy: free, wild, untethered.

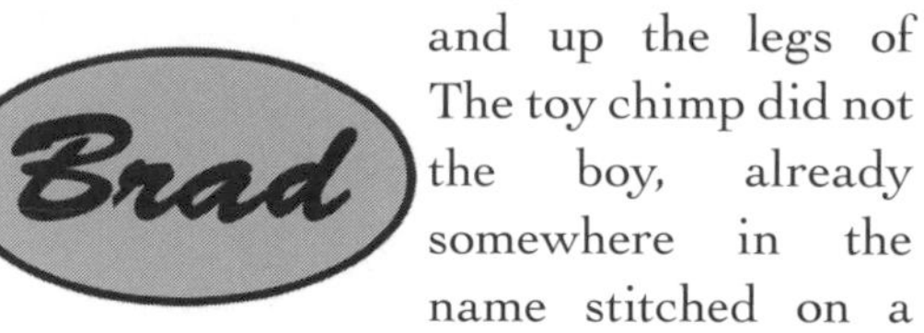

Eventually the boy grew taller and lost interest in Mister Butcher's crotch. But Mister Butcher's mouth...

O chimpanzee mouth shaped hollow!

...that is another story.

¶ SOME THINGS GIRLS SHOULDN'T TALK ABOUT.

I am 51 years old, Mother, I am not a girl. I am vice president of a major telecommunications company. My male staff refers to me as Big Bad Ball Buster behind my back, and I like it.

¶ SOME THINGS WE JUST DON'T DISCUSS IN POLITE COMPANY.

You are not polite, Mother. You are rude to cashiers and waiters and children with loud shrill voices. You are rude to me.

¶ SOME THINGS ARE BEST KEPT TO YOURSELF.

Why, Mother? So I, like you, can pretend I'm a better person than I really am?

¶ ACT LIKE A LADY.

Your husband, lady, had a mistress for 35 years, and he hated you so much for nursing him when he was ill that he shat in the bed though his bowels worked fine, and when he died you felt such tremendous relief you hummed gospel music while you ate dinner alone, using your fingers to tear meat from bone and your shirtsleeves to wipe the chicken fat from your face.

But of course THE DEFENDANT'S WIFE will never say that. Her mother is 78 years old. She knows that if the old woman finally were to admit her world was disadvantageous, prejudiced against her will and pleasure, she could no longer exist, for her existence is based on a belief that she is not archaic, that she lived the best life she could have lived. The thousand other options that lay just beyond the edge of her reach were swept under the rug years ago.

FIFTY-SEVEN $100 BILLS SEWN TO THE UNDERSIDE OF HER LIVING ROOM RUG. MONEY QUILT, SECURITY BLANKET, SAFETY NET. SHE HAD SAVED FOR A RAINY DAY, A STORM, A DELUGE. BUT THE FLOOD LAY BEHIND HER NOW. AHEAD NOT A CLOUD IN THE SKY: SHE DIED IN HER SLEEP.

OVERSIMPLIFICATION #1: THE DEFENDANT'S WIFE *is a hypocrite*.

She tweezes iron-black whiskers from her chin, taking pleasure in the stinging pain. Today she's resigning as vice president of a major telecommunications company to save her marriage of 26 years, a marriage wrought with mutual abuse, infrequent and unsatisfying sex, and two children she thinks would be devastated by divorce but who pray for one so they'll receive twice as many Christmas and birthday presents, just like their friends. *Pluck!*

And on top of everything else some plastic surgeon in Connecticut won the $97 Million Powerball.

THE DEFENDANT peeks out through the living room curtain, searching for the mailman, then ambushes him before he reaches the front porch. THE DEFENDANT has done this every day since he ordered Enlargo® from www.penis-online.com. Today, again, there's nothing but bills and credit card solicitations and magazines and.... He is so goddamn sick and tired of Publishers Clearing House telling him he's won $10 million dollars if he holds the winning entry. Tired of watching his wife search through Publishers Clearing House pile of shit product fliers for stamps she's got to tear out and lick and paste on the entry form in order, she thinks, to improve her chances of winning. Tired of his wife ordering magazines like *American Astrology* and *Consumer Reports Money Adviser* and *InStyle* and *Town&Country* and *People* and *Parents* and *Health* and *Shape*, the house littered with goddamn liberal media lies. A goddamn terrorist could be working for the shitbags who print the sheets of order stamps; they could put cyanide in the glue and thereby kill millions of Americans stupid enough to keep playing a losing game.

THE DEFENDANT imagines his wife licking another Publishers Clearing House stamp as if it's a big fat juicy dick. Imagines her moaning in pleasure. Imagines her strutting to the mail box like she's already won. And what the hell would she do with $10 million, anyway? Probably leave, quick as a horny hell hound. Probably quit her job and move to some tropical island like... like...um...Brazil.

THE DEFENDANT punches his right fist into his left palm and mumbles, "If Dave Sayer ever knocks on our door, by God, I'll fuckin' pound him!"

And on top of everything else, the economy's going straight to the shitter.

WORKING FOR WOMEN

Complete our COMPATIBILITY PROFILE *and find out today!*

A. Circle the highest education level completed:

YOU	YOUR SPOUSE
1. High School	1. High School
2. Bachelor's Degree	2. Bachelor's Degree
3. Master's Degree	3. Master's Degree
4. Ph.D.	4. Ph.D.
5. Post Doctorate	5. Post Doctorate

–3

B. How often do you and your spouse have sex?

+5 points	Every day
+3 points	3-5 times a week
+1 point	1-3 times a week
-2 points	Fewer than 3 times a month
-5 points	Sex? What's that?

–5

C. ADD ONE POINT where you and your spouse have the same taste.
DEDUCT ONE POINT for each area where you differ.

– Movies
– Books
– Music
– Sports
– Politics
– Religion

–6

And on top of everything else there are rumors of lay-offs.

At the end of the seven days, the waters of the deluge covered the earth; and Noah went into the barge along with his sons and his wife and his sons' wives, driven by the waters of the deluge.

— Genesis

In seven days THE DEFENDANT's WIFE will go to work for a man who once worked for her to whom she twice denied a raise on grounds of insubordination. She will earn $46,850 less than she earns now but still $2,945 more than her husband. But she will tell him $5,945 less. He will know she is lying. They will argue. All hell will break loose. And now, uh-oh, this whisker's gray. She silently tallies her savings, investments, pension plan, IRA. Again. She knows she has her own deluge, but hers is dead ahead.

She can see it coming.

She can smell it coming.

I Want To Satisfy My Lover. How L-O-N-G Should I Be?

THE DEFENDANT pulls a bottle of men's cologne from the glove compartment and splashes it on his neck. His coworkers think he wears too much scent. They call him a faggot and amiably spank his ass and pinch his cheek. He used to tell them to fuck off but now he says nothing. Just stares at them mean-like and pictures their eyeballs popping out of their heads as he strangles them one by one. He used to wear cologne for his wife but now he wears cologne for the girl who works the food truck. She's pretty and twenty-something and has great tits that she shoves his way every morning, saying, "Mmm, I could smell you coming, Brad." To which he replies, "I only come for you, darlin'." He's sure if he could fuck her just once he'd get back to his old self again.

And suddenly the windshield's a movie screen and he has this mental image of his wife trying in vain, trying in fact with some desperation to suck him to a hard-on. He, as audience to his own chagrin, clenches his jaws so tight his teeth screech. To delete the image he slaps himself hard across the cheek four times, then splashes on more cologne to soothe the sting.

    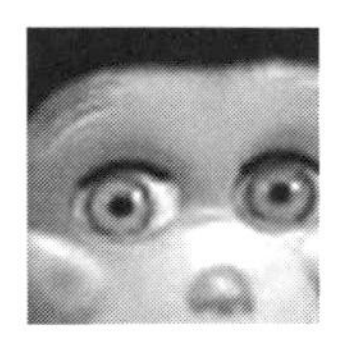

OVERSIMPLIFICATION #2:
The Defendant *__is a cliché__*.

THE DEFENDANT"s quality of emotional life is based on the quality of his penis's life. Right now his penis is sad, pathetic. It slumps. Feels inferior to other penises, especially the penis of the top dog, big boss Jirí Cêch, though he's never gotten close enough to actually measure the boss's dick. Not that he hasn't tried. Once or twice on a job site when Jirí Cêch left the Porta-Potty unlatched and the wind sucked the door wide open, **THE DEFENDANT** saw him pissing but his back was turned of course, and the shadows were too deep. Nevertheless, he deduced that Jirí Cêch must be hung like a goddamn elephant by the way he leaned back when he pissed, as if to keep the weight of his dick from pulling him into the shitter. Besides, how could anyone with a small dick be as cocky as Jirí Cêch, a foreigner to boot, from somewhere in the fucking nowhere of Europe, a commie most likely, spying for Russia or the Taliban or Saddam, and sure as hell a goddamn liberal since he reads *The New York Times* and listens to National Public Radio in his SUV. He suspects his wife is a goddamn liberal too, though she claims to vote Republican. Once, when his pickup was in the shop again, he borrowed her car and found a copy of *The New York Times* in the back seat. She claimed a colleague had left it for her because of an article in the business section about their up-to-no-good-as-ever CEO.

BUSINESS/FINANCIAL DESK | February 12, 2003, Wednesday

For Sprint Chief, a Hard Fall From Grace

By SIMON ROMERO (NYT)

KANSAS CITY, MISSOURI - Critics say Sprint Corp's financial performance in recent years provides justification for board's decision to force ouster of chief executive William T Esrey and president Ronald LeMay, even if their tax shelters had not become targets of Internal Revenue Service inquiry; Sprint spokesman Bill White says Esrey will continue in his position until company succeeds in hiring Gary Forsee, vice chairman of BellSouth and chairman of its Cingular Wireless joint venture with SBC Communications; Esrey's career at Sprint discussed; chart; photos (M)

* Source: *The New York Times*

<u>YOU</u> Are In Total Command

He: *"You're lying, goddamn it!"*

She: *"No I'm not, just look!"*

He: *"It don't matter if the article's there or not, I'm saying it's your goddamn newspaper!"*

She: *"And I'm saying it's not."*

He: *"And I'm saying you're lying."*

She: Bites her tongue and cries. What she always does when she wants to scratch his eyes out with her manicured fingernails.

He: Sneers, *"Fucking crybaby bitch."*

ABSOLUTELY TRUE TESTIMONIAL
"Before I was always embarrassed, but now when I go workout or even just take a shower I feel really proud. For real, Enlargo has turned my life around. I'm amazed that a little pill can do all this!"
—B.J., Missouri

OVERSIMPLIFICATION #3: The Secretary ***<u>is always the smartest</u>*.**

THE DEFENDANT's WIFE's crazy morose SECRETARY with breast cancer puts the resignation letter on the desk.

"I left in your grammatical errors," says the SECRETARY. "For old time's sake."

"I should fire you," says THE DEFENDANT's WIFE, "for old time's sake."

"Yeah, but you won't," says the SECRETARY, lightly, almost energetically. "Just like you won't leave your fucking loser of a husband."

THE DEFENDANT's WIFE flushes red, but she can't decide if it's from rage at the offense, shame at the accuracy, perimenopause, or a combination of the three. Regardless, she wants to stab her SECRETARY with the shiny brass letter opener she's never used for anything except cleaning her fingernails. "You know nothing about my husband or life."

The SECRETARY crosses her arms over her double mastectomy as she always does before she begins a diatribe. "I know you believe the only way you can tolerate this corporate hole you've dug for yourself is by being married, which you think somehow defines you as less a loser than your unmarried sister, no matter how much your marriage sucks."

THE DEFENDANT's WIFE reaches for the letter opener.

"And," says the SECRETARY, "if you left him you think you'd lose your mind because then the charade would be over and you'd have only this shitty well-paying job, and your hair getting grayer, and your tits and ass sinking lower, and young MBAs eager to topple you from your high horse, and Human Resources looking for a way to early-retire you so they can save thousands of dollars in salary and benefits. You'd have, really, nothing at all to live for and so you'd probably kill yourself instead of looking a gift horse in the mouth."

THE DEFENDANT's WIFE thinks the SECRETARY's spiel sounds way too familiar. "You little bitch, you've been reading my email."

The SECRETARY laughs. "Every time you go out of town."

THE DEFENDANT's WIFE raises the letter opener. Lets sunlight through the 18th floor windows glint upon its smooth surface. "I'd be doing you a favor if I killed you right now," THE DEFENDANT's WIFE thinks she thinks then realizes she has said it aloud when the SECRETARY goes white.

"But I'm in remission!" bleats the SECRETARY.

"Well," says THE DEFENDANT's WIFE. "Lucky you."

She sets down the letter opener, stands, slips into her suit jacket, grabs her copy of *The New York Times* and calmly states: "I'm going to lunch. Please take the rest of the day off because I don't want to see your little smirk when I get back."

GOOGLE

Search Results:

	2004	2006
goddamn liberals:	984	1,170
god damn liberals:	342	94
goddam liberals:	122	566
godamn liberals:	7	5
godam liberals:	5	1

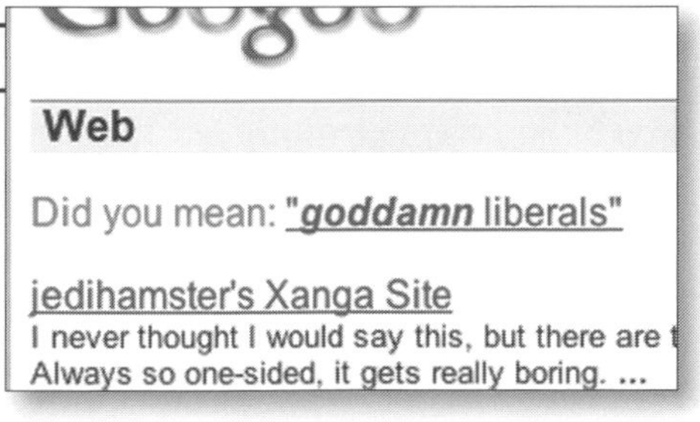

Web

Did you mean: "***goddamn*** liberals"

jedihamster's Xanga Site

I never thought I would say this, but there are

Always so one-sided, it gets really boring. ...

And on top of everything else
the economy's going straight to the shitter.

And on top of everything else
Rush Limbaugh is in rehab.

OxyContin Addiction Help
1-800-942-2056 ▸▸▸ Free Legal Consultation
Contact Us Here

Do <u>YOU</u> Want To Be Better Than "Average"?

ABSOLUTELY TRUE TESTIMONIAL
"I can stay hard as long as I want and I never come too fast. I used to have a real problem with that and felt like a loser. Now with Englargo I can ride any woman as long as she wants with no problems at all."
— I.P., Louisiana

"Hey, Brad!" yells one of the guys.

THE DEFENDANT steels himself for the inevitable wisecrack to follow.

"Did you just burp?"

"Fuck off," THE DEFENDANT yells over his shoulder.

"You musta burped," yells another guy, "cause we smell dick!"

That's it! Last straw. Burr under the saddle. Titanic's iceberg. Joshua's last trumpet wail. Bottom ace yanked from a house of cards. THE DEFENDANT picks up his pneumatic nail gun loaded with 59 screw nails and charges like a barmy bull. The guys scatter, giggling and swearing and hooting. THE DEFENDANT chases one after another, aiming his gun like a cowboy. Then he trips over a 2'x4'. Falls headfirst into a skanky puddle of mud and machine oil and whatever-shit.

Will There Be Any Side Effects?

Red light. THE DEFENDANT's WIFE squeals to a stop behind a Champagne-colored Lexus SUV. She fishes a pack of cigarettes from her briefcase and lights up. She thinks her husband thinks she quit three years ago, but he knows she still smokes: He can smell it on her clothes, in her hair, on her breath from Dunhill clouded lungs. Almost $6 a pack now. She wonders if she'll have to switch to an American brand after her salary reduction. The possibility depresses her. As if on cue, thunder claps and the sky pours. She slumps back in the heated leather seat and sees a new billboard above a strip of dilapidated apartment buildings.

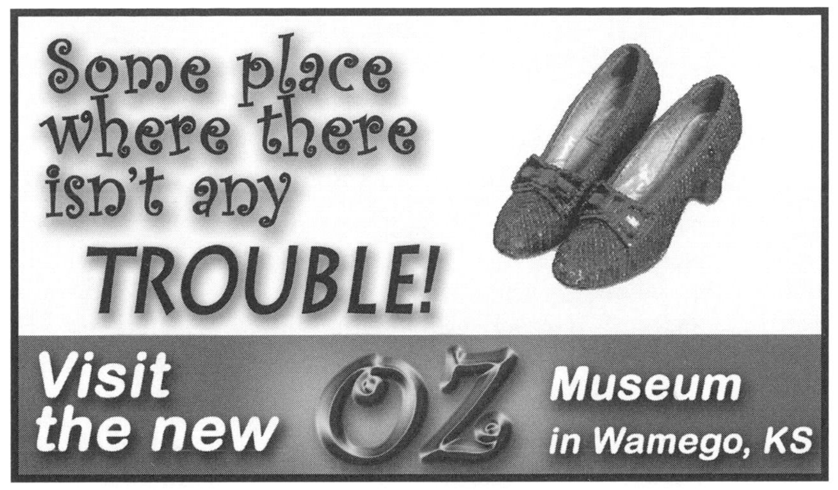

Her favorite movie is still *The Wizard of Oz*. Once upon a time she saw herself as Glinda, the beautiful good witch of the North. Her fiancé, Brad Roberts, who would eventually become her husband who would eventually become THE DEFENDANT, she saw as the Lion: all goofy, strong, cuddly—and, in the end, a *hero!*

"The Lion?" Brad had complained. "He's a freakin' homo!"

"No, he's not," she'd giggled, a sand grain of political correctness chafing her conscience.

"Freakin' chickenshit homo," Brad had repeated, hoping to get another giggle from his wife-to-be. But she had only looked down at her bare toes, so he'd said, "I want to be the tornado." She'd given him a puzzled look, so he'd said it again. "I want to be the tornado."

Now, after 26 years, THE DEFENDANT's WIFE sees THE DEFENDANT as one of the Wicked Witch's hideous blue winged monkeys.

Sees herself as Glinda with a smoking and drinking problem.

And on top of everything else
the traffic signals are fucked up:
This light will not turn green.

How BIG Can You Get?

Downpour! THE DEFENDANT thanks God in whom he no longer really believes—though he invokes God's name whenever the goddamn liberals want to pass some goddamn law protecting fucking pervert homos or lazy fucking welfare moms or fucking blacks too fucking stupid to get an education or fucking Mexicans sneaking over the border taking American jobs...

"Who you talking to, Brad?" asks the food truck girl, and she laughs, her tits jiggling so hard they almost fall out of her little scoop-neck tee-shirt that's getting damp from rain spray and thus semi-transparent.

"Oh. Ha," is all THE DEFENDANT can think to say as he stares at her nipples. Then, weakly, "Didn't you smell me coming, darlin'?"

"Honey, I sure did!" she says, wrinkling her little nose. "What happened? You fall into the Porta-Potty?"

THE DEFENDANT raises an arm and sniffs. And, indeed, even the rain can't wash away the puddle stink.

"I..." is all he can think to say before the girl looks past him, her smile stretching wide and she stands straight and touches her hair, her lips, an earring, her neck.

"Hi, bossman!" she calls.

THE DEFENDANT turns to see Jirí Cêch growing bigger as he saunters toward them, impervious to rain or dirt or fatigue or even time. Jirí Cêch grins, winks at her. Slicks back his hair. Then Jirí Cêch looks at THE

DEFENDANT—who feels suddenly too short, too young, too old, too bald, too small, too everything that Jirí Cêch is not—and Jirí Cêch says, "What's that fucking smell?"

And on top of everything else they're saying Noah was an African and his sons three different shades of black.

"Nobody has any patience anymore," sighs the black cop, hands on hips, scowling at the fallout from the collision. The Champagne-colored Lexus SUV ahead of THE DEFENDANT's WIFE tried to sneak through the eternal red light just as a Pearl-White Ford Explorer SUV came barreling through the eternal green light, and now there's Champagne and Pearl everywhere, and shattered glass and blood mixing with the rain on the pavement, and it'll be 45 minutes at least, says the cop, before they get the intersection cleaned up and traffic moving through, and there's no backing out, either, because some jackass talking on his cell phone plowed into the back of the rear car, a Golden Cashmere Saturn, that was consequently rammed into the Victory Red Pontiac Grand Prix in front of it that then twisted sideways into the other lane where it was hit squarely by a Toyota Tundra pickup painted Desert Sand Mica that was trying to sneak through the intersection by going the wrong way down the left lane. THE DEFENDANT's WIFE, whose Mercedes is in the middle of the fray, stomps her shoe on the wet asphalt and says, "Uh!" And the cop repeats louder, more slowly, "Forty. Five. Minutes. Ma'am."

She wants to scream or cry but instead sees an antique store across the street and goes shopping.

And on top of everything else they still haven't found the WMDs.

Results That Are <u>BIG</u> For A Price That's Low.

THE DEFENDANT buys a 12-pack on the way home and guzzles three before he arrives. He slams the pickup door and tromps into the house, boots tracking mud on the carpet and hardwood floors. *Tromp tromp tromp.* Slow pounding beat of a primitive drum. Doors slamming. Beer cans spewing. Dog yelping. Cat hissing. Every gesture an opportunity for noise, cruelty, brutality. He punches the answering machine: His wife has a meeting, she will be late, he'll have to get his own dinner. He screams, "God damn it!" almost a wail, and throws a full beer can like a fastball in no particular direction. It cracks the plate glass window particularly in the living room. He inspects it, thinks it resembles the path of his life—straight and narrow but with no discernible direction.

Then:

The mailman arrives!

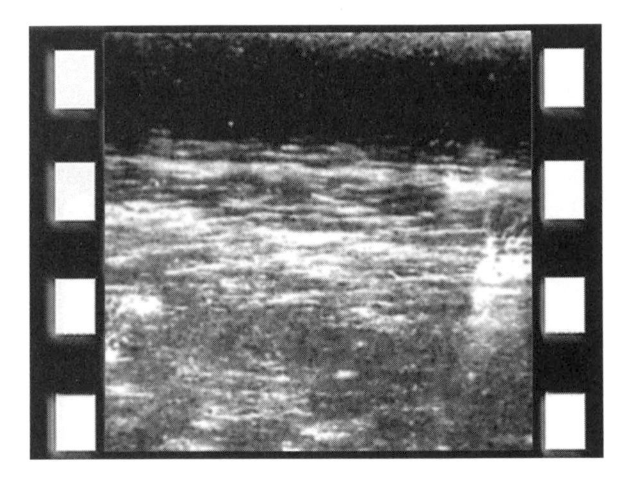

It's all out of order now. We can't seem to establish the correct timeframe. Either THE DEFENDANT or THE DEFENDANT's WIFE is lying, or the events leading up to the crime were so mesmerizing that time no longer mattered to them.

THE DEFENDANT's WIFE went shopping, an activity that often leads to critical memory loss. In the antique store she found a stuffed toy chimp dressed in red plaid shorts with a plastic banana fused to its right hand. The banana fit perfectly into the chimp's mouth. "Cute," said THE DEFENDANT's WIFE. She said it again, "Cute." And then she thought, *If I cannot see my husband as anything but a primate, then maybe I can imagine him as a cute chimp rather than an ugly monkey. This marriage will work!*

Sometime later THE DEFENDANT snatched the box of Enlargo® from the mailman, rushed into the house, and immediately swallowed two pills. He went to the bedroom to watch his penis become colossal. There, in the middle of the bed, lay Mister Butcher. THE DEFENDANT would never know if the massive hardness of his penis was caused by Enlargo® or by Mister Butcher's familiar beckoning mouth. Nor would he understand the demented rage that surged through him when the doorbell rang just as he was about climax.

When the front door opened, DAVE SAYER of Publishers Clearing House saw a naked man sucking on a plastic banana fused to the hand of a stuffed toy chimp wearing red plaid shorts and suspenders. The chimp hung from the man's mouth, its dingy-white plastic sneakers bouncing on the substantial erection of the man's substantial penis. DAVE SAYER's photogenic smile froze on his face. Nevertheless, he summoned the savoir faire to ask, "Are you Brad Roberts?" before THE DEFENDANT let loose an eerie simian cry and raised a tightly balled fist.

ON THE RUSHWIRE:

David Limbaugh Reports from Rehab: *Rush Doing Great, Not Becoming Liberal*

My grandmother DIED
without ever having an orgasm

Don't let it happen to YOU!

Sponsored by
INTERNATIONAL SOCIETY
OF WOMEN WHO BELIEVE
IN BIOLOGY

MACHINE GHOSTS

Am not I
a fly like thee?
—William Blake

THIS BLUEBOTTLE FLY HAS NEVER seen a human. Never drunk the bald primate's oil or spit or salt. Ate its shit. Laid eggs in its soft rotting flesh. Here no worlds collide. Wind's hollow by the time it reaches these old black gum and bur oak and hickory trees writing rings of time in their wooden hearts. Water moves. Sun lights. Prairie grass bows to creatures with hearing so keen that fungus spreading's like thunder a quarter-hour away in spring.

And so I am ready. Some little death a gap through which to squeeze my splendid soul.

Buzz loudly!

No one swats or complains.

Not even the black she-bear licking her bleeding paw. Smell the sweet oozing stench! Find the wound! Leave your squirming cosmic mark, your opalescent legacy, your hungry lovely holy white maggots of God!

CALLIPHORA VOMITORIA!
CALLIPHORA VOMITORIA!
CALLIPHORA VOMITORIA!

O how fleeting's life.

MIDNIGHT IN SUBURBAN K.C.

THE POET Jirí Cêch has fallen in love with THE IDEA of Emily Dickinson.[38] Or so he says, standing at the hotel window, waiting for his one concert of one to begin at one, watching jets descend on Kansas City's airport 20 miles extant in the hideous hinterlands where nonpareil architectural design remains unpronounceable, certainly unconsidered, considered not at all except unmarketable as if it were a new vacuum that didn't suck. He/You there/Czech-in-Love fallen who once claimed, "Having sex with virgins is like dry-humping a kayak," humming.

"Besides," he says, slicking back his black hair[39] there at the window where there's no visible distinction between a Boeing *727* and a bluebottle fly pummeling itself against the pane, "I don't fuck local journalists."

---

[38] On the other hand, THE REAL ESTATE DEVELOPER Jirí Cêch is still in love with THE BODY of Jessica Lange playing Dwan better than Fay Wray playing Ann Darrow in *King Kong*. Jirí has frozen poor Jesse there, in collapsible time and space, as only a vampire can: See how perky still her breasts? How dewy yet her skin? How hopeful ever the sparkle in her eyes as if she were her own lighthouse for a world about to shipwreck on the craggy shore of the future. Oh, Jessica! Jessica! Even the obtuse beast is mesmerized by your dazzling presence, your bright-and-shiny-object-ification-ness!

[39] And the Jewish girl with blue ribbons in her black hair? You loved her most, you once said, recalling all the women and girls with hair exuding pheromones in every breeze and you in throbbing-hot pursuit from downwind. You once said you loved her interminable. Loved, you said, her there in that place where ghosts and ghosts-to-be (you and we) come together tangling sighs with/in each other, scentless seamless winds. We do not wish to beat a dead horse, but is she now only sunken memory or you only a liar? The ribbon's not even dust or ash, just the gleaming fabric of time folded in upon itself in the mud of hearts obscuring all we suspect but won't confess: *I too murderer.* What is it we share, if not the crimes of history—our burden, our rusted yoke? For even we cannot help but love the exterminated girl *and* her ashes ever descending, cheek of flame all that's left of Jewish daughters in your choked dreaming of throats clotted with sludge from the boots of soldiers marching weary-sheepish to their slaughter. And ours. Lest we deny the mortality to which we're obliged.

Did we say we wanted [—*to engage in sexual intercourse with*—] you?"

"You didn't have to."

And he turns then, grins, and we recognize the searing flame of famine in his eyes when he says, "Sweetheart, I can smell the wet between your legs like fresh truffles on the back of my bloody tongue."

MEMORANDUM

Date: January 30, 2005
From: Gerald Peterson, General Manager
To: Staff
RE: **Spicin' Up the News**

In an attempt to boost ratings, I am instituting format changes **immediately**. These will include a zippier logo (see above), cooler computer graphics (we are borrowing styles from current Hollywood blokbusters, such as "The Matrix," and awesome audio like the zooming sound of bullets in "CSI: Miami," for example. Our outside consultant, Richard Stadelman, whom some of you have met, will be meeting with each of the primaries this week to discuss how to improve your appearance and news or weather delivery, as well as making between news chitchat more entertaining and warm & fuzzier.

In the meantime, Richard has provided a list of words and phrases to incorporate **immediately**. Our writers and reporters are expect to saturate stories with these attention-grabbers. We want viewers to get **EXCITED!** when they watch our news, **no matter what we're reporting on**.

Now, we're here at...
Just a few minutes ago...
Earlier this evening...
Live at the scene...
Let's go live now to....
Exclusive report...
Only on Four...
Late-breaking coverage...
The latest news on...
Happening now...
Up-to-the-minute...
Right now...
At this time...
Most recent update...
We're on the scene at...
We'll keep you posted...
We'll keep you up-to-date...

Shocking story
Gruesome details
Horrific events
Ghastly crime
Grisly scene
Frightening events
Feared for her life
Terrified witness
Terrifying events
Anxious residents, students, etc.
Startling realization
Alarming incident
Disturbing news
Troubling situation
Distressing news
Worried parents, citizens, etc.
Nervous residents, etc.
Panic resulted

TV 4 Reporter: Now, when most people think of Kansas they imagine wheat fields and vast prairies rippling in the inexorable wind. They picture sunflowers tilting round yellow heads toward a shifting sun. Perhaps they envision airfields of Boeing jets since the company's headquarters are in Wichita. Or maybe they think of... Czechoslovakia?

The maggot is aware of the trials that await it. Deep inside its cells endures an equation only the God of Flies can solve. Yet now I witness the purling light inside my sacred pustule of flesh.

The Poet Jirí Cêch: No one, not even Herr Hitler himself (herself on days he wore lederhosen, a touch of rouge, nipples pellet-hard as he *heiled* limp-wristed as if carelessly shooing flies, mare's tail swatting on a hot summer day), no, not even *der Fuehrer* could part hair as straight as Emily's. Tidy line demarcating left and right hemispheres colliding in doubt about God, life, but never death for which she ached *'Tis not that Dying hurts us so—'Tis living—hurts us more—* when ached her corpus from what killed her. *And dander like tiny cherry blossoms fallen upon your black hair that I'd inhale or arrange pretty on my temple if only you'd rise from death more flesh than words.*

TV 4 Reporter: Well, we're here right now, in the middle of Bohemia's resurrection. Wilson, Kansas. *Acht!* I have never seen so many goddamn flies in my life! Can somebody get me a fly swatter? [*—inaudible from off-camera—*] What!?! I thought we were rehearsing!

DOCTOR OF MEDICINE
SAMUEL J. CRUMBINE

of Dodge City tried to save Kansas from its scourge of flies by urging citizens to install window screens in their homes. They say he created the slogan, "Swat the Fly!" after attending a baseball game where flies lodged in the eyes of short-stops and fielders ran after fly balls and crowds chanted to batters, "Swat the ball!" Oh, yes, it all made sense, and so when schoolteacher Frank Rose showed Crumbine his "fly bat," a ruler with a square of wire mesh attached, the good doctor renamed it "fly swatter." Sadly, Crumbine could not foresee the colossal corporate pig farms and cattle feedlots stinking up the 21st century landscape, filling water tables with shit and piss: stewpots of fucking flies fucking flies.

REAL ESTATE DEVELOPER
JIRÍ CÊCH

takes a room at a motel in Limon, Kansas, the tiny town where he hopes someday soon to connect the suburban sprawl of Kansas City to the suburban sprawl of Denver. Upon entering the dank room he exclaims, "What a fucking shit hole!" He sees a fly swatter on the nightstand and assumes a maid has accidentally left it behind. He picks it up with two fingers and throws it out the door, into the parking lot. That night he dreams poetic of Emily Dickinson tickling his lips and nose with her eyelashes. An intense humming swells in his ears and he has a wet dream. He wakes in sticky darkness to find his face and hands covered with flies and suspects he has died and gone to hell. Still breathing in Limon, he is half right.

"We're going back to the 1880s. It does make us look to the people in the rest of the country that we're a bunch of hicks."

— Charlie Pierce, biology teacher at Hutchinson High, commenting on the Kansas Board of Education's vote to drop evolution as a subject in the science curriculum.

TV 4 Reporter: Well, we're here, live, at this instant, in the middle of Bohemia's resurrection. Wilson, Kansas! Where a truly shocking story is about to unfold right now in our exclusive report. Nervous residents of this sleepy little town, also known as The Czech Capital of Kansas, are awaiting the arrival of real estate developer Jirí Cêch. Now, we're told that Cêch has traveled all the way from New York to meet a man who claims to be the son he never knew. Even more startling is the nervously anticipated arrival of a woman who claims to be Cêch's childhood Shiite baby shitter...er, *sitter!*

The Poet Jirí Cêch: *Kolache, vanocka,* just shake your head and make all the worms tumble out.

I could not die—with You—
For One must wait
To shut the Other's Gaze down—

Unable to go back to sleep, he loads his hookah with opium and smokes himself to delirium. An adolescent fly alights on the cinderblock wall. He presses a fingerprint of cum onto the slippery beige paint. The fly hesitates, then crawls to drink.

O my pretty insect! My Poetess of Carcass and Corpse!
Bending now so lowly small I see my own fraught eyes
shimmer in your belly's blue.

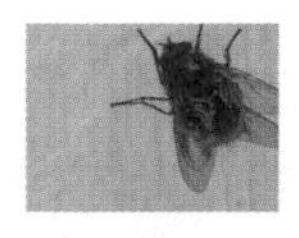

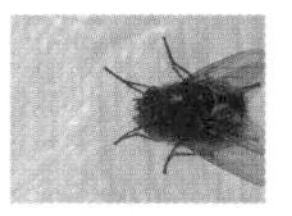

"Why do you mention her?" ***Who?*** **"The Jewish girl."** ***Because the name of your concert seems incongruous with your emotional past.*** **"My concert has nothing to do with the girl."** ***But Dachau...?*** **"She died at Auschwitz."** ***But isn't it...?*** **"No."** ***And isn't Emily...?*** **"Another story."** ***And yet the ribbon...?*** **"Blue as the sheen of the bottle fly's belly."**

O My Dachau Darling!

(what'd you eat today?)

I just *love* Versace & Death!

LIVE!

the real Jirí Cêch™

with

Pyuria

Rockin' Finnish Death Metal

CALLIPHORA VOMITORIA Tour!

Rejected by Cannibals

Exclusive Fashion Week Performance!
February 6, 2007 at Memorial Concert Hall Arena
For tickets call Tikitme®
816-444-9310

Not an endorsement of or by Versace or any of other Fashion Week sponsors, designers, advertisers, participants, or their silly little pets.

What the maggot denies itself quivers at the edge of every issue's fate. For I am master of this race toward oblivion. I suckle the bloodied teats of beasts. Gnaw gorgeous in my lurid bloat.

Like Ground Zero...

Twenty years ago in Paris while researching a biopic on Danny Cohn-Bendit[40] I briefly shacked up with a North African biochemistry student in his one-room apartment equipped with sink and mattress and hot plate and small rectangular window through which nothing appeared but varying shades of winter gray. He said he was 24 though his driver's license indicated 26. He said he was Muslim but drank wine to excess. He said he preferred me without makeup but ogled women with eye shadow and lipstick and rouge. In the morning we drank espresso and fucked. In the afternoon we ate lunch and fucked. In the evening we smoked hash and fucked. Always, when I'd bend over to pick up my panties he'd grab me by my pelvic bones and fuck me from behind. Fast and forgettable except for his irrepressible monkey-want. He wouldn't allow me to reach orgasm, wouldn't let me touch myself. I'd secretly masturbate in the dirty community bathroom down the hall, standing with my back to the locked door, my ass blocking the keyhole. Once he said, "I am your master, you are my slave," and slapped me. Not hard. But a slap. The next day he left for school (he said) and I left for Italy (I said). For years afterward he managed to track my movements. Sent brief, intense love missives. Still referred to me as, "My baby." His postmarks originated from Berlin, Rome, Madrid, Cairo.... Wherever he went, bombs exploded.

When the maggot's love liquefies the skies rain cold sand. I hear the trees screaming, the grass bones snapping, and my earth's a black river between stones. God's voice stands outside my Self and commands: "Curl and Fold, O Hallowed Maggot! Live to shout my furious name!"

The [r]Evolution Has Begun

> ***Was crucified, died, and was buried. He descended into hell. The third day He arose again from the dead and ascended into heaven and sits at the right hand of God the Father***

---

40 After the May 1968 student uprisings in Paris, Cohn-Bendit earned the moniker Danny-le-Rouge for his left-wing politics. Subsequently, and consequently, he was thrown out of France, taking up residence in Germany where he found influence in the Green Party. Now known as Danny-le-Vert, Cohn-Bendit became president of the European Green Group, winning a post in the EC parliament. Meanwhile, the U.S. Dollar continues its precipitous decline against the Euro and the Yen.

Almighty whence He shall come to judge the living and the dead.

—from The Apostles' Creed[41]

HERE, IN THIS UNSULLIED WILDNESS, FEW adult flies live through cold winters. Those that do survive by sinking into a slumber so deep not even the smell of shit can wake them. Not even the smell of shit-eating pigs eating shit and shitting shit before spring comes and the *trifolau*[42] turns the sows[43] loose to search the woods for the sexy smell of truffles they'll root out along with bluebottle pupae buried sleepy and ripening in the fine black dirt.

The maggot is a power in this world like no other: Ordained to turn flesh into water, to irrigate with vomit the soil of perpetual life. Change the corpse to seed, seed to flower, flower to nut, nut to feed the corpse-to-be in this rectangle of life with me its magnificent god's eye.

DIRTY FILTHY LUCRE

In Japan, Hitachi makes "Clean ATMs" that press yen between hot rollers for a tenth of a second at 392° to kill bacteria for hygiene-obsessed Japanese. A study published in *The Journal of Forensic Sciences* found that 100% of U.S. $20 bills held traces of cocaine. Another study found that 42% of paper money harbored objectionable germs such as fecal bacteria and staphylococcus aureus.

HE KEEPS EMILY'S PICTURE[44] IN HIS WALLET, BEHIND HIS GREEN CARD, WORN NOW, THE PICTURE, THE CARD, FROM THE UNITED

---

41 "The earliest universally accepted Christian creed is the Apostles' Creed. It was formulated by Christian leaders in the first century of the faith, i.e., about the year 100 or before, and is still in use today. This creed protected true believers during the dark days of the catacombs—the terrible persecutions which dogged Christians throughout the event that the Book of Revelation describes as the 'first battle of the End.'" (*Source:* www.jesuschristismygod.com)

42 Italian for "truffle hunter."

43 Dogs as well as pigs are used to hunt truffles; pigs are more eager to find the prizes, but it can be difficult to keep the pig from devouring the truffle. Only sows are used—the smell of Italian white truffles (*Tuber magnatum Pico*) contains pheromones that are attractive to female pigs, but not to boars. (*Source:* http://members.tripod.com/~BayGourmet/history.html)

44 Picture of Emily Dickinson surreptitiously extracted from the wallet of Jirí Cêch, scanned, hand-painted, and embedded, a term now more typically referring to, *exempla gratia*, a freelance journalist for *Rolling Stone* embedded with the U.S. Army's First Calvary Division out of Ft. Hood, Texas.

What does it mean to suffer? Can it be this perpetual chill, all light doused, the thunder of feathered wings over-head? Is there no end to pain? Let me sleep. Wake to dawn. Heat spilling along these branches like honey-sap.

STATES OF AMERICAN PRIVILEGE OF FONDLING TWO-DIMENSIONAL OBJECTS ENTHUSIASTICALLY.[45]

Do you think she ever masturbated?

"Who the fuck knows?" says Jirí, violently searching the mini-bar for Pilsner.

A reclusive but obviously passionate woman.

"Pabst Blue Ribbon?! Ick!" He pops the top anyway. *Pfftth!* "And how come this hotel don't got no cable TV?"

It's interesting to speculate on what she did all those lonely hours in her bedroom, writing poetry about a dead lover and her lover Death.

"Fucking remote doesn't work and—*Whoa!* The anchor people have two serious cases of helmet head!"

www.eff.org/br/

I didn't mean to make you wicked—but I was—and am—and shall be—and I was with you so much that I couldn't help contaminate.

---

[45] Except child pornography, the possession of which carries heavy fines and time in prison wherein grown men once buggered to madness now wait for your big fat pink dimpled ass to *schlumpf* through the steel door, dead man running the other way too late, should've thought of that before you forced boys to suck you off in the church bathroom, in the public park, in the school locker room, in the rec center, in your SUV with photos of moist adolescents —somebody's children beasts of burden—under your driver's seat, ink jet on cheap paper bleeding now with cum. And you, no the other you, Refugee-from-Love-and-Soviets You, Jirí Cêch, were only 15 when You too took it up the ass/in the mouth for a decent meal, maybe a beer or three beforehand so it didn't hurt as much, not just pain in the ass which You could tolerate, tough guy that You weren't but quickly became, but also in Your soul You call Your Little Biting Fly searching for a place to land after it flew and left Your gorgeousness hollow. And this American land You now ravage with houses blanketing blackening this land like fly specks... Houses sealed so tight and sanitary from truth not even the Calliphora vomitoria can survive a hot summer meal inside... It's not home here, no, never was/will be, just a hotel lobby with revolving doors through which they all come and cum: Your lovers nameless and flesh-torn and keening *O save me from my mortal memory! Let me wallow in the muck of two-dimensional drugs and three-dimensional windows against which my soul hammers itself silly to break free: Death always the lover waiting in the wings.*

How To Masturbate

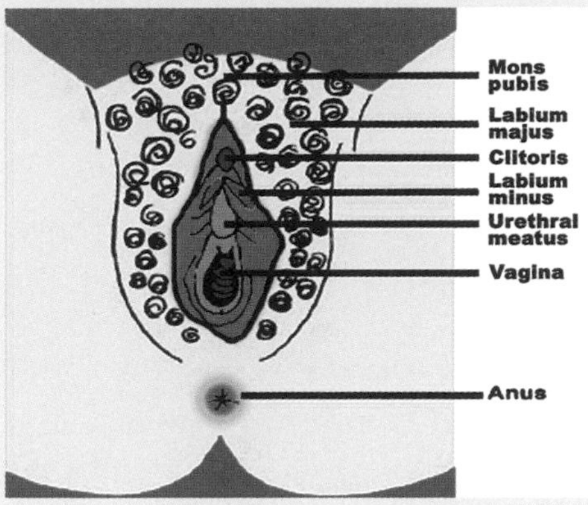

Dedicated to those parents in the Kansas Blue Valley School District who are incapable of intelligently discussing with their teens the topic of masturbation.

Don't be ashamed to use a mirror to familiarize yourself with your vulva (also referred to as your "genital region"). Like race, religion, culture and disabilities, we tend to fear and sometimes loathe what we don't understand. Your vulva is a gorgeous creation! Get to know it and appreciate it.

The clitoris is the most sensitive part of the female anatomy, with thousands of nerve endings – many more than the penis. Hooray! Because a clitoris is so sensitive, direct or prolonged stimulation can be irritating, sometimes painful. That's why a circular motion that crosses over the clitoris and includes the labia (also called "lips") may be more pleasurable. Wet your fingers with your own vaginal fluids or KY Jelly to reduce disagreeable friction. Other finger motions to consider are (1) vertical, repeatedly crossing over your clitoris, down to your vagina and back up; and (2) horizontal, repeatedly crossing over your clitoris by moving your finger side to side; or (3) a combination of any and all.

Every woman is unique, which means that your vulva will be as distinctive as your face.[46] Your preferred methods of sexual stimulation will be unique, too. That's why it's important to learn what feels best by exploring your body with enthusiasm, like we did in the sexy 60s and 70s vs. the Double-Ought-Naughts.

Finally, don't forget to help your partner discover what makes you feel good. Faking orgasm cheats no one but the faker and lets inept lovers think they're great in bed.

---

[46] Unless you've had plastic surgery in order to look like one of the identical losers on *The Swan*, forgettably freakish flounder with lips filled fat with collagen, and tits oozing silicone someday soon enough, and big blue plastic butt implants sagging at 70.

Would she even have known how to masturbate?

"Who, the anchorwoman?"

No, Emily Dickinson.

"Don't taint my image of her."

And indeed, except for the blue ribbon, Emily's photo is now grayer: lights darker, darks lighter, caught, she is, in a state of in-between-ness. And see: hair pulled so tight her brow's arched in righteous rebuke.

O naked worm, legless and blind! How just to be chosen! What wonder to behold my diaphanous skin, furuncle of fat! All deaths are created for my pleasure, my feasting, my frenzied celebration of Alpha in an alphabetic world.

The Poet Jirí Cêch: What's pity but the brute's conceit? Man with a cigar, thrice as big as his dick, guffawing, *That poor sap,* while inside his colon disease spreads faster than slick shit in rain. Dead man running without legs below the knees. And if we're really nothing but the words we speak, then you my Poetess Fair are *ever* and *majestic* and *sublime* to brazen out the maggot's breath, to let the *Calliphora vomitoria* tread upon your lacrimal caruncle, footprints sunk in desiccating tissue.

while my lover was, he said, at school, I swept dead flies[47] from the narrow sill into the palm of my left hand. Their weight was less than a tickle on my skin. Hollow brittle. Legs and legs and legs crossed over thoraxes as if the Holy Father of Flies Himself had laid them all to blessed rest.

And I felt sad. And I felt afraid:

The sky seized nothing but its unspoken emptiness:
A dead fly does not fly but falls:
The voiceless do not sing:
This is not love.

And what rough beast, its hour come round at last,
Slouches towards Bethlehem to be born?

—W. B. Yeats

47 "[Bluebottle flies] are potential disease transmitters and particular pests of the meat industry and slaughter houses, commercial canteens, food preparation areas and even domestic kitchens." (source: www.sentrypestcontrol.co.uk)

FROM BUTTERY FLUID AND BUNDLES of nerves the cosmos forged the bluebottle's wings like leaded glass, eyes like garnets or the well-fed red-brown blush of Guatemalan babies. Yes, this salty sarcoplasm of muscles that fly the fly its first flight above the moist fecund earth. Last year, in the Era of Godness, the Penultimate Age, the Ancestors ascended from World as if from death and mated upon the thistle, driven toward the pleasure of cells, the ecstasy of synapses, mystical metaphysical egg-and-seed of godhead. Whence the 120 sons and daughters that begat the 120 that begat the 120 and so on and so forth until the summer's end and the tribe of five million million was accomplished.

Here, from half a mile and more around, come we in the lovers' season, our tryst sanctified by the sun. Feel, Lover, its light heat your blue to a metal hot sheen.

Think of it, lover! I and thee
Permitted face to face to be.

BEHOLD THEM ENTERING UPON THEIR PROMISED LAND,

THEIR REEKING PARADISE[48]

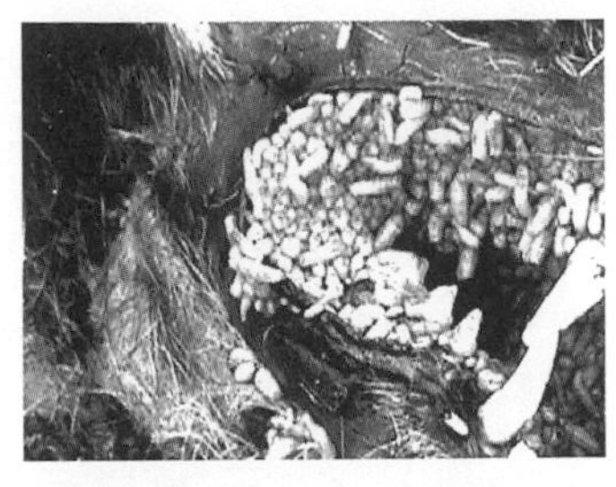

NEITHER GOOD NOR BAD THIS WORLD of sun and heat and ripening stink. World only "World" to the shimmering fly, her ovipositor stabbing and stabbing the juicy meat, planting her eggs like a frenetic gardener. Ah, this flat handsome Eden, without rival! Plain plane of plains overwhelmed by the healthy wealth of this immodest creature whose right to flood and ravage is divine. And if this thing of life and death knew the forgotten wars of hairless beasts it would dream nostalgic of the putrid murdered, battlefields a bacchanalian banquet, drunk it would ever be on the torn and blasted flesh of the human dead and dying.

What a gorgeous mouthful! What an idea! Some beast of the apocalypse here to bring you mercy! If you are the ending, I am the beginning. From my matchless citadel of muck and worms, watch me rise!

TV 4 Reporter: Well, we've got late-breaking news here in Wilson, Kansas, with the most recent update on our exclusive TV 4 story. Now, uh, it seems that a number of angry residents from various political and religious groups have converged on Wilson to protest what we can only assume is the, uh, eminent *[sic]* arrival of Jirí Cêch, his allegedly gay son...or, uh, he may be Cêch's brother...and his allegedly, uh, uh, Shi'a babysitter.

The Poet Jirí Cêch: Dear Emily, Were you a fly on the wall of this 727 flying over this bitter-ugly-barmy heart of my country of exile, quilt of green irrigation circles[49] splayed flatter than

---

48 Jean Henri Fabre, from *The Life of a Fly.*

49 "In arid western Kansas, the fertile prairie has been transformed into [a green] oasis of sorts since the introduction of irrigation technologies after World War II. By the 1970s, most of the water had been appropriated and an agribusiness industry based on irrigation became entrenched.... The data indicates parts of the Ogallala aquifer will be used up within the next 25 years and vast tracts of land will have no usable groundwater in the next 50 to 100 years." Subsidence of aquifers is irreversible. (*Source*: www.uswaternews.com)

Calista Flockhart's chest, you'd see metal wings tip downward as the scales tip out of balance and we descend, silly prideful deluded beasts of the Reckoning, into the hole we've dug so deep there's no way out now, no resurrection, only vanishing into vanishing until the last man remaining's a combat zone for maggots and grubs.

TV 4 REPORTER: Now, we told you earlier, in our exclusive report, that the babysitter was Shiite. Well, we've received numerous statements from anxious residents that the babysitter may in fact be Sunni. Now, all we know for certain is what's been relayed to us, exclusively, by worried citizens, that the babysitter's religion starts with an S and is, presumably muslin. Uh, that is [—*looks down at notes*—] ... uh ... Moslim.

O hideous little bat, the size of snot.
—Karl Shapiro

To purge the earth of death's impurities, that is my divine purpose.

Really, isn't Emily just your latest obsession in a long line of idées fixes? Some whim that comes and goes, in and out of your consciousness like a winged insect through a cold, dark-lit room?

"Want a cashew?" asks Jirí. "Incredibly, they're not stale."

The poet bored of living dead, so loving the living dead—Emily with her clever dash of pause and breath, little here-to-there line demarcating the fat-swarming world here she inhabited there on her page in her mind, that line a slit through which she'd slip, like a finger between labia, and all the wetness of creation a swooning banquet of word-interlaced silence?

"Hey," says Jirí, trying to snap his fingers but not succeeding and therefore staring at the failed hand, slipping it into a trouser pocket, fondling coins, penis, scowling at the untimely itch and hanker. A moment passes with nothing but the slackened whining of a fly at the window. "Hey," Jirí repeats, "I wonder if the musicians from Pyuria have arrived yet? I'm feeling a little bit lonely and somewhat desperate for validation. I need a round of golf." [50, 51, 52]

Knowing, as you do, how mean and safe to love the dead! How simply, uh, you know, uh, heroic.

Americans & Europeans spend $13 billion a year on perfume[53]

In the hotel lobby three quiet boys with long hair stand fidgeting with their *Calliphora Vomitoria Introitus* CDs, practicing Finnish acquired online, waiting for Pyuria band members to exit the elevator, hoping to get autographs.

"Hei, herra. Sinun musiikki on iso! Miellyttää allekirjoittaa CD!"

---

50 "Veteran [golf] pro Tom Watson, whose [first] wife and children are Jewish, resigned from the Kansas City Country Club last year after it blackballed accounting mogul Henry Bloch, a Jew. Although the club changed its mind about Bloch, Watson did not rejoin. In a *New York Times* column last month, he decried the 'hypocrisy' of admitting a single black to 'integrate' and urged, 'Let's discriminate right now, each one of us, privately, between what is right and what is wrong.'" (*Time*, July, 1991)

51 "I'd like to get two bull terriers and walk them across Kansas City Country Club and let them shit on the greens," said fiction writer James Ellroy, in an interview at www.crimetime.co.uk.

52 Why do I feel the need to leave trails of facts to prove that *Homo sapiens* have come not far at all, that racism and sexism and classism and etceteraism thrive here in this Red State rubble like flies in the nostrils of dead Iraqi soldiers, hidden, those flies, but still feeding fatly on mucous and blood? And as if to confirm some pattern of which only a corner is revealed, a male cardinal sees its reflection in my window, mistakes it for a competitor and attacks, knocking itself unconscious while somewhere a father blames his whole rotten luck on the women in his life, something he states quite clearly in the note he writes before blowing his brains out with a Winchester shotgun.

53 The amount of money it would take to meet the world's food and sanitation needs.

Finally, the elevator door opens and the quiet boys stand straight and hopeful. But it's only a young neo-Nazi wearing a big-ass swastika on a red shirt, black armband around his skinny bicep, hair buzzed short, pimples picked bloody, teeth off-color and leaning this way and that. This boy, let's call him Dwayne, has spent a month's wages to fly to Kansas City for the annual Aryan Nations convention—not *the* Aryan Nations but yet another extremist offshoot for wretched boys of all ages unable to find a place of unconditional love and acceptance even among Jew-haters and African-American-haters and Hispanic-haters and Asian-haters and Other-haters...[54] unloved, unaccepted, as in their furious broken—*kaput!*—homes with parents careless-poor or ignorant-stupid or both and wretched wretched wretched[55] in so many fucking ways subtle and blatant that to list them here would force you to think entirely too hard about *why* things are precisely *what* they are, now,[56] why men will be boys and boys will be boys: lonely, afraid, clawing at that next rung on a worm-eaten ladder that doesn't go anywhere, is just a rotten ladder rising from a blue ribbon in the muck and mire, not even high enough for a pretty view of sky. *Fuck!*

---

[54] He'd name the Others, that new Nazi boy, if he knew history or social studies, but he was never a good student, everything so hard and sleep-inducing, and he feared always the teacher's eyes upon him, expecting, expecting, expecting...what? Some miracle? Some kind of goddamn breakthrough, as if his skull would suddenly crack open and all his dumbfuckedness would just fly away like winged bugs and then he'd know everything quick and sure and would get rich fast and leave mean-ass dad and whiny-ass mom and drive a red Trans Am or Grand Prix along a hot beach where blue-eyed blondes with big tits waved at him like they meant it, *Sieg Heil*, Dude, fucking *Sieg Heil!*

[55] *[—begin rant—]* Oh, *really*? Sure, once upon a time skinheads roamed the night streets of London, sons of electricians and plumbers, wearing Doc Martens and white tees and suspenders and tattoos, disaffected youth infected by their parents' (Dad's, usually) furious refusal to believe they are in any way responsible for their low-slung lives, must be the fault of ***Jews with money*** or ***Blacks with big dicks*** or ***East Indians working three or four shitty jobs at once***. Anyway, that was then. Now, it's the American middle-class whites joining up, meeting secret in that suburban house down the street. Mr. Stasis, Mr. Mundane, Mr. Middle-Rung, Mr. Debtor, Mr. Is-This-All-There-Is leaving pig shit on my front steps because my husband's half-Jewish with a whole Jewish surname (I'm an eighth Jewish myself, but they don't know that because I took my surname from my first husband, an Italian-Argentine, and they can't distinguish between Italian and French, and my eyes are Aryan blue, yes, and my skin's pale). And now even the pathetic local news is onto the white supremacists, smoking them out of their white collar →

Which is what Dwayne says to the three quiet Pyuria fans standing simultaneously disappointed and astonished in front of him. Says fuck not loudly, no, rather under his breath. But still an *F* is unmistakable: white man's overbite: teeth on the bottom lip. And the breath that follows: *uhh!* And the hard *K.*[57]

And one of the quiet long-haired boys, let's call him Brian, says, quietly, "Fuck who?"

And Dwayne thinks, *What would Hitler do?* And then says, "Fuck you, fag-head."

And Brian wonders, *What would Pyuria do?* And then says, "Haul the black future towards us!"[58] And inside that seemingly empty but highly volatile space between one boy and another, between buzz-cut and long hair, between Death Metal and Military March, between red shirt and black shirt

The vivacious animal always goes forward, chewing, swallowing, digesting until the earth's dissected by trails of waste toward which the stupid eagerly draw near. What I find hideous they find habitable. O pity their deeply lowly nature!

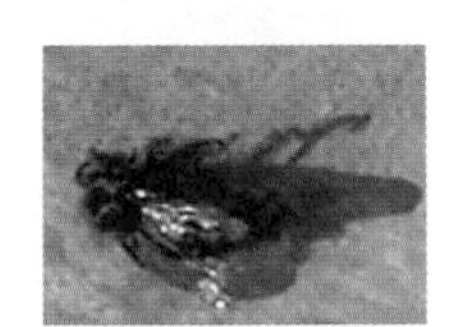

a fly dies. Falls from ceiling to floor. But no one notices.

---

jobs, their white clapboard houses, their white neighborhoods in their white counties, and half of the viewers are thinking "Oh, it's not *that* bad," and the other half are thinking, "Where do I sign up?" and I'm squished somewhere in the middle, not telling you half of it, no, I refuse, because you're clueless, *clueless*, you hear? You live in your delusional enclave of educated see-no-evil monkeys, agreeing to agree on a human optimism that raised Hitler to power and lowered 11,000,000 people to their fly-specked deaths, while German cognoscenti sat around smoking cigars and drinking imported cognac and discussing Hegel's concept of "human being." And never mind Rwanda, Bosnia, Iraq, Somalia, the Sudan, Indonesia, China.... You said, "Never mind the fucking genocides, the clever killing of genes. The way we huddle in tribes," you said, "reminds me of overfed maggots in a flood of piss and shit—if you catch my highly aromatic drift." [*—end rant—*]

56 "Photos posted on the [National Socialist Movement's] web site show members gathered at the Berliner Bear, a German restaurant in south Kansas City. About 30 men and women were dressed in uniforms with swastikas. One picture is of a cake with the message, 'Happy 116th Birthday Adolf Hitler.'" (*Source: The Kansas City Star*, May 3, 2005)

57 On January 25, the Kansas Supreme Court set down a ruling that made Kansas the first state to legally oust the [Ku Klux] Klan. But that was in 1925. (*Source:* http://www.kshs.org)

58 *Source:* Pyuria (www.pyuria.com)

fly specks[59]

[59] Approximately 40,000. The estimated number of children who starved to death today.

Jirí Cêch rises before dawn to escape the plague of flies swarming even the shower, lapping cum and sweat and tap water stinking of this State's vile excreta as if those embittered reactionary men and women with their opposition placards *[anti-this/anti-that, pitypit/pitypat]*, their squinty eyes, their self-subjugation loathing, their blue ribbon veins popping, their scary skeletons knocking/pounding from inside subconscious closets, oozing now and then and now again as something base, freakish, barbaric[60]—Judeo-Christian God not even a facsimile of facsimile in their Aryan blue eyes,[61] just a tribal shield against—as if they've all shit their hatred into the hollow stocks of lilies of the fields of the plains of this nation under God indivisible, say they, never asking who the hell's god would despise so much The Other, their Other who lives across the Line[62] wherever drawn in dirt or tar or DNA, skulking in the shadow of their simpleton nightmare.

60 The BTK ("Bind, Torture, Kill") serial killer was president of his Kansas church, and everybody sez, as they always sez, "He was a nice guy, quiet-like." And don't you wonder, don't you ever the fuck ask *why* it is these killers were so often embedded deep in the church, a church, any church that would look the other way lest someone look too closely back.

61 In March 2005, the national director of Aryan Nations moved to Kansas City and rented a P.O. Box, thereby making KC the national headquarters. In April 2005, The National Socialist Movement—"an organization dedicated to the preservation of our proud Aryan heritage and the creation of a nationalist socialist society in America and around the world"—held its annual conference in Kansas City.

62 State Line Road between Kansas and Missouri: fine line, color line, white line. red line, **blue line,** Jew line: "Most of the [racial] restrictions—including those in more than a dozen subdivisions in the Country Club District [of Kansas City, including my own neighborhood]—prohibit ownership by blacks, but some Johnson County [Kansas] covenants are even more exclusionary. The 'Declaration of Restrictions' for Leawood Estates filed by Kroh Bros. in 1945 prohibits ownership or occupancy 'by any person of Negro blood or by any person who is more than one-fourth of the Semitic race, blood, origin or extraction, including without limitation in said designation, Armenians, Jews, Hebrews, Turks, Persians, Syrians and Arabians.' An exception is made for 'partial occupancy by bona fide domestic servants employed thereon.'" (*Source:* Judy L. Thomas, *The Kansas City Star,* February 13, 2005) On March 31, 2005, the State Senate unanimously passed an anti-racism amendment requiring homeowner associations whose covenants contain language once banning minorities from owning or renting property to remove the restrictions. But that was in the State of Missouri.

Jirí Cêch steps naked into the parking lot to retrieve the fly swatter, dirtier now with oil and dust, the swatter is. A couple from Wichita, dressed synthetic and on their way to a holiday in the Rockies, stop dead-ish in their tracks, mouths agape: (1) Husband dumbstruck by the size of Jirí's enormous penis in this chilly morning air, which is all the man sees—PENIS![63]—and then head swells enraged by a fluttering desire in his own swelling groin, some long buried signal rising like smoke from a dead-cinder soul; (2) Wife dumbstruck by a man so handsome;[64] she shrieks through her nose when two breeding flies alight on her upper lip.

> *[T]he small gilded fly*
> *Does lecher in my sight.*
> *Let copulation thrive...*
> —William Shakespeare

TV 4 Reporter: Now, we're live again, in Wilson, Kansas, where, as you can see behind me, the street is crowded with protestors on all sides of a lot of different fences. And tensions are rising. It's amazing that one man could cause so much fear, anger, even hostility as protesters clash over stances ranging from religion to politics to sexuality to race and fashion.

The Poet Jirí Cêch: Those many years you sat at your bedroom window studying each weightless corpse of flies dead after a long, futile hammering against glass: gate between heaven and earth, let's call it—striving toward there from here, and the glass though liquid refusing to bend or break. I know you loved more, as I do, those shattered wings and dusty eyes than the still-dewy scutellum of the young. I know you would love, too, more dearly than my dearest lovers my aging soul loveless witness to human

---

63 The memory of it hereafter the conductor's baton that will start Husband singing Jesus songs, especially in the shower.

64 Handsomeness hereafter Wife's image of Adam before the Fall from grace, and sure, if God must manifest in flesh then He would be more beautiful than Gabriel, wouldn't he, no matter how many flies He swats, maniacally, upon reentering the hotel room, not "God," of course, but "His Handsomeness"?

misery and succor and clinging to gods neither compassionate nor impartial nor smarter than some women, you, beloved, Emily, dear, heart.

TV 4 Reporter: Yes, you heard right. *Fashion!* As you can see, the group calling themselves The, uh, Cool Extreme is, at this very instant in time, involved in what can only be called a screaming match with The Uncool Militants. And as you can see by our exclusive coverage here in Wilson now, it's basically a battle between people who wear black and people who wear, uh, somewhat dingy shades of pastels and earth tones. [*—looks at her dress—*] I seem to be wearing blue.

Ground Zero...

I last heard from my long lost North African lover in a message left on my answering machine. He said, awkwardly, the years having devoured as much of his English as his life, "My baby. I am in Kansas and I think of you and our nice days in Paris still. Please call me at the number of my friend. I would like again one night like in Paris when first we had the love." After I summoned the courage to call, the phone only rang and rang and rang and rang and rang.

That was yesterday.

I did not try again.

What matter of life is this? My butter churned to wings, to black legs unfolding under my indigo gown. And now I see what it was to be blind, to only suckle without grand view of my ascendancy.

THE FIRST CHILL INSTRUCTS THE FLY of its imminent dying. This, too, recorded in nucleic acids: Words in the Book of Life. The warning bell tolls, signals the fly to flee. But there's no place to go. The sun is setting. And it will die tomorrow anyway, having laid its eggs in the she-bear's wound, nothing more to contribute to this marvelous world. And, yes, what marvels here now vanishing: blood of maple sweet and dust of pollen sprung from plants that smell of rotting meat. Electric storm! Magnetic sun! What glory there is to witness the dance! To dance this one reel before the melody stutters and the musicians at last and ever lay down their reeds and horns.

The Movie You've Been Waiting For!

Jirí Cêch walks into town, spurs jingling, coat flapping like a black flag in the wind. He's so fucking tired of this Red State road, dust rising under his boot heels, harmonica wailing from some tar-papered rooftop melting in heat. He says, "No one ever tells you how hot it will be, how it will feel like your eyeballs are melting in their sockets, your tongue swelling fat and purple as an eggplant shoved down your throat, your skin sloughing like asps." He wants to stop. Wants to maybe take a seat on the front steps of the Wilson Opera House, light up a cigarette, think about a girl he once knew, years ago, before he was born: the way her blue ribbon caught wind and light and life woven like a double helix around her black curls, fair neck: the way her critical eyes looked through you into a future entirely cleansed of her laughter: the way her little wave and words—*Auf Wiedersehen!*—ascended from the flue of history and lodged under the wing of a bluebottle fly en route to suppurating meat: the way the fly suckled, trees leaned, soil inhaled rain...

The wish is realized. Let a new covenant issue forth like vomit from the mouths of maggots, for we are made in the image of our God. His omnipotence shines in our blue flesh.

But there's no stopping now.

Everyone is waiting.

Terror becomes them.

For what power do they possess but their sad bloated fear?

> ***Life, when all is said, is a knacker's yard, wherein the Devourer of today becomes the devoured of tomorrow.***
>
> — Jean Henri Fabre[65]

---

[65] And I was nothing more than a footnote, unread, on a page in the history of a world before me and after me, one parasite on one Saprinus grub that feeds on one maggot that feeds on one human that feeds on one planet in a solar system only one of 200 billion in a galaxy only one of 125 billion in a universe that may be only one of many or none at all.

TV 4 Reporter: *[—breathless—]* Now, we are live right now in Wilson with this late-breaking, exclusive report on what will likely be, uh, the biggest story of the year, if not, uh, the century! As you can see behind me, uh, uh, all hell is breaking loose as opposing groups come head to head on virtually all of the, uh, all of the hot-button issues facing us on the political horizon today, right, uh, now, and, oh, oh, speaking of horizons! If you look just beyond the sign that reads, "**I HATE EVERYTHING**" you can catch a glimpse of Jirí Cêch who as one frightened resident said, is, uh, [—*reading from notes*—] "like the pied-piper of protestors, calling all the rats into our village." Now, we don't know for sure if Cêch's arrival is, uh, really, uh, the cause of all this, this, disturbing unrest, but what I *can* tell you is that...uh... uh... Wait a minute. Just a minute, please. I'm getting a signal from...uh...there's a noise...uh...oh!...noise?

Zero...

After wine and hashish and unsatisfying sex, I asked my lover what, exactly, he studied all day, why before eating he washed his hands obsessively, scrubbing with a stiff-bristled brush until his fingers nearly bled. He sat silent a long while, then brought out a small briefcase full of glass vials. In the vials were bluebottle flies, pupae, maggots, eggs. And he said:

> *If thou wilt not let my people go, behold, I will send swarms of flies upon thee, and upon thy servants, and upon thy people, and into thy houses: and the house hall be full of swarms of flies, and also the ground whereon they are.*
>
> —Exodus

WHEN THE GROUND REACHES A CERTAIN TEMPERATURE a new generation of flies[66] hammers through brown papery coffins and crawls out of dirt. A haunting silence precedes ascension: time, a magnificent rancid kingdom of the dead. Nadir to apex, the final trinity: *Maggot, Pupa, Fly.* And oh oh what ravaged splendor awaits them! And oh oh how they hum in exultation!

> *The fly sat upon the axel-tree of the chariot-wheel and said, What a dust do I raise!*
>
> —Aesop

Cloud of flies, cloud of dust, cloud of fire over your head as you approach the end of another Bohemia.

"Fuck," says Jirí Cêch, watching people flee from him, their personal Beelzebub,[67] "I guess this means my concert is cancelled."

and then
There interposed a fly,
With blue, uncertain, stumbling buzz,
Between the light and me...

[66] And what a coincidence, isn't it, that just as I near the end of this story my husband starts receiving neo-Nazi emails at his office from some rabble in Germany who write that "multikulturalism is multikriminalism" and "Europe must deport Lebanese children and teens" and "*Augen Auf! ya ya! Augen Auf!*" and it makes me want to brush my teeth till my gums bleed.

[67] Translation: "lord of the flies"

FLY FLYING FROM THE FUTURE TOO SLOW it realizes too late. Realizes, above all things above all else, what it is: no more and no less than a small gap in the world, one gap of infinite gaps, holy hole in absence as in being, belly sheen an everlasting memory in DNA that will not veer from hungry form, unlike that soft bipedal putrescent beast below, guts laid open, writhing, that knows and is startled by the last vision of all visions—fly and sky—and their shared utterable peculiarity:

It is a little late, O my pretty insects! Yes, it is a little late. Night descends: last glimpse of moon in that persistent void. Should we die before the Sun's tonic revives our stiffening wings, let us not be forgotten! Dear Mother of Life and Egg! Father of Death and Seed! Let our lust for living manifest in a Heaven of endless death and rot!

And then the windows failed, and then
I could not see to see.

. . .

My foreign lover had drunk so much wine that night, smoked so much hash that he slid to the floor, propped up by the white wall. His head nodded like a junkie's. His snore rose like a death rattle from his slow-heaving chest. A fly landed on his pretty brown cheek and he jerked awake. Gazed at me from deep inside his sleepy stupor. Sadly smiled. Said, "My baby, oh my god, what we do with the life." And fell asleep. We were so young then.

∞ The she-bear sits on the zenith of the highest hill above this placid verdant valley. Her wounded paw healed long ago: no crust of scab marks it, no pink scar. Healthy bear, she will live many years and die without pain. But now, here, in this redolent Eden, she sways, eyes heavy-lidded to what must be the music of setting sun, rising moon and night wind thick with extravagant scent and chortling things. What is she thinking, there on the hill still warm from late summer's day? That ripening ruby red sun-bleed, what is it she loves so about its final, seamless glow?

NOTES:

1. The first phrase or sentence of each "Fly Bible" passage (marginalia) is appropriated from Jean Henri Fabre's 1920 book, *The Life of A Fly.*
2. Text inserts in blue italic are from Emily Dickinson's poetry and correspondence. Exceptions are the blue dedication in "How To Masturbate" and blue words or phrases in footnotes.

Forget Botox®

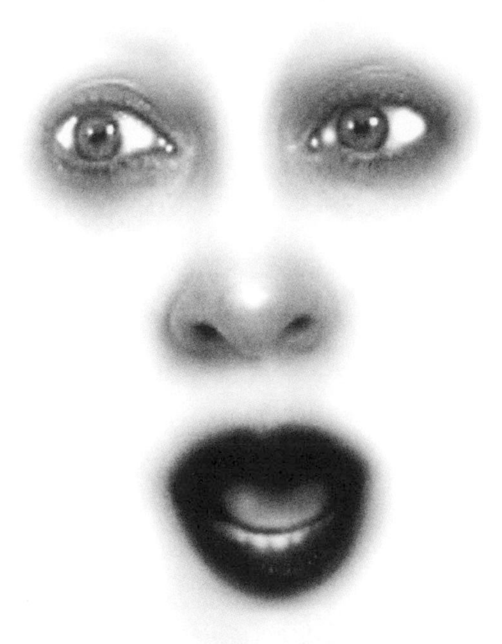

Let us inject you with the Ebola virus

There's only one way to avoid the ugly signs of old age: Death. Wrinkle creams, face lifts, acid peels and botulism can make you look terrific. For a while. But sooner or later you're going to look exactly like a used Fendi handbag that's been pissed on by a homeless, syphilitic drunk and then left out to dry in the Palm Springs desert. And all the plastic surgeons in the world can't help you. But we can. Just one painless injection of Ebolife® will have you looking like an angel in no time. But don't wait. Call us now. Cause you're getting uglier ever minute.

the real Jirí Cêch™

capitalist consumer *products!*

More than 300 fabulous creations of art therapy drawings, experimental poetry, art & music DVDs, CDs, clothing & lots & lots of absolutely *must-haves!*

the real Jirí Cêch™ says:

"Don't be an ugly bastard! **BUY MY STUFF** and become *instantly* attractive!"

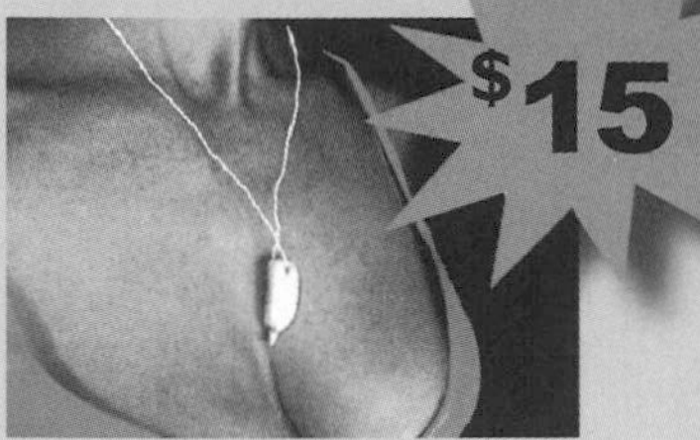

$15

REAL Dessicated Garlic Pendant
strung on dental floss! Keep those damned bloodsuckers away!

These items come nicely packaged!

$12

***WHITE* Gravel!**
from one of Jirí's suburban sprawl construction sites! Signed and numbered!

$8

Paper Bags
for drinking Pilsner in public!
(C'mon! You know you need it!)

Made in USA!

Kül Magnets & Ass Patches

4 ~~2~~ dots R gööder then 1

who is
the real Jirî Cêch

$5 to $10

$35

Concert Posters!

And the real <u>*REAL*</u> POPULAR:

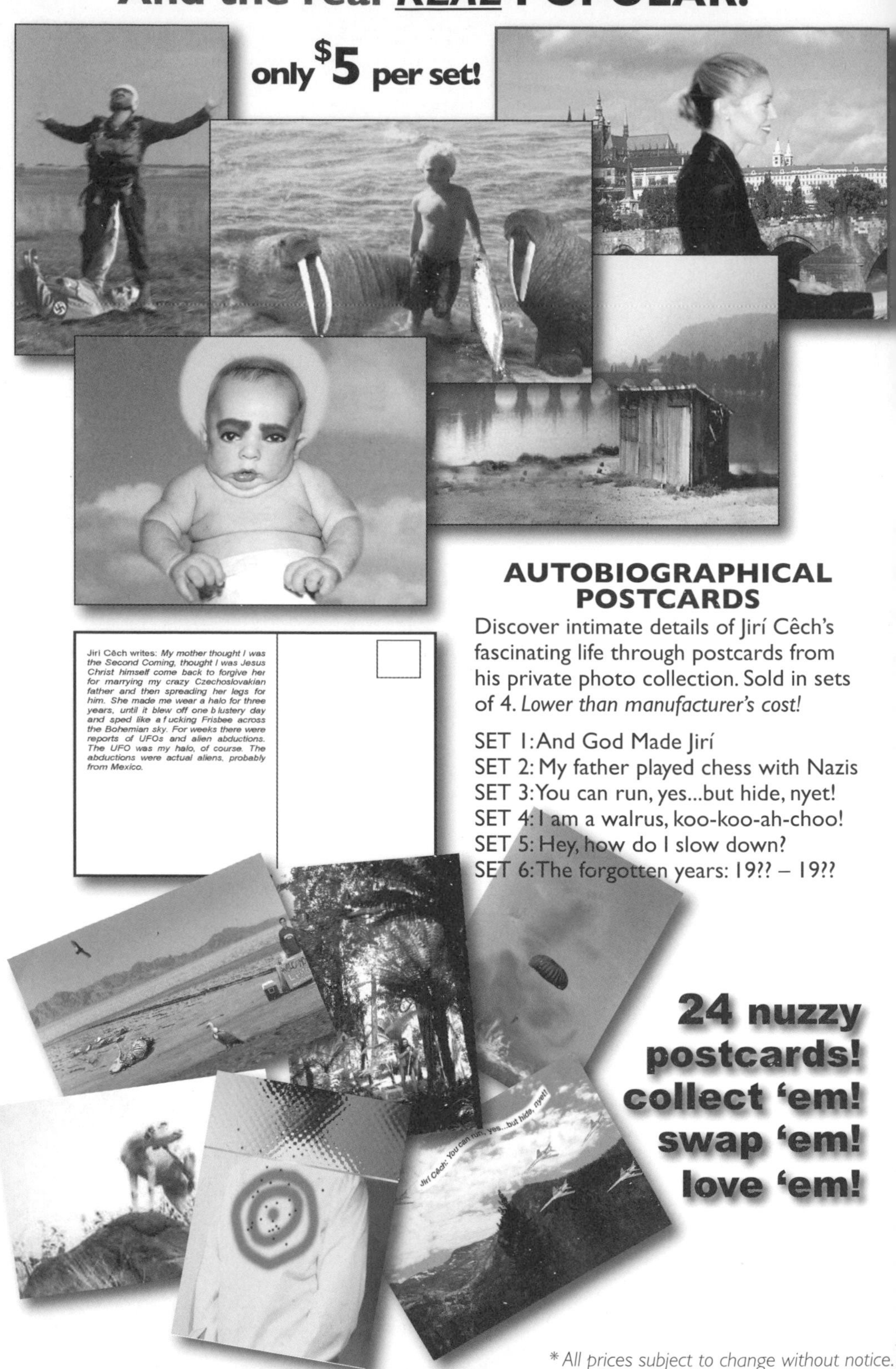

** All prices subject to change without notice.*